Edward Bruce Hamley

# Thomas Carlyle

An Essay Reprinted from 'Blackwood's magazine'. Second Edition

Edward Bruce Hamley

**Thomas Carlyle**
*An Essay  Reprinted from 'Blackwood's magazine'. Second Edition*

ISBN/EAN: 9783744749787

Printed in Europe, USA, Canada, Australia, Japan

Cover: Foto ©Andreas Hilbeck / pixelio.de

More available books at **www.hansebooks.com**

# THOMAS CARLYLE

## AN ESSAY

REPRINTED FROM 'BLACKWOOD'S MAGAZINE'

BY

## GENERAL SIR E. B. HAMLEY

SECOND EDITION

WILLIAM BLACKWOOD AND SONS
EDINBURGH AND LONDON
MDCCCLXXXI

# PREFATORY NOTE.

THE death of Mr Carlyle has been the occasion
of a renewal of those controversies respecting
his merits as a philosopher and a writer, which
his works, as they appeared, always excited.
The tone of many of the obituary memoirs in
the public journals has called forth grave objection as too entirely laudatory. As in the
present Essay an endeavour was made to trace
his philosophy through his most important
works, and to estimate them without prejudice,
it has been thought that, though it appeared
many years ago, its republication at the present
moment may be not inopportune.

# THOMAS CARLYLE:

## AN ESSAY.

---

## MIRAGE PHILOSOPHY.

No one of Mr Carlyle's disciples, we should think, ever became a Carlylist at once. The singularity of style at first puzzles or repels—the persevering reader then finds some suggestive idea which leads him on—in time the obscurity clears up, the images and ideas shine through, causing what was distasteful to appear admirable—till, finally, the dubious student, no longer perplexed by the cipher of which, as he flatters himself, he has discovered the key, becomes the uncompromising champion.

But a great number of readers turn back on the threshold, repelled by the startling aspect of that singular phraseology. To them he is merely affected and obscure—even if they have gone far enough to disentangle a leading idea, they perhaps recognise it as a truism in masquerade, and set him down as a charlatan. His writing appears to them to be, as Sir Hugh Evans says, "pribbles and prabbles—it is affectations."

Between these two classes—the knights who see only the golden side of the shield, and the knights opposite who are blind to all but the brass—we should like to strike some sort of balance of opinion, and find between the oscillations a firm stand-point, from whence to survey the History of Frederick—a History marked in its outward aspect by all the strongest peculiarities of the writer.

At the root of all Carlyle's works lies a main idea in a particular aspect. The idea, he tells us, he derived from the transcendental philosophy, as expounded by Fichte : it is this—

"That all things which we see or work with in this earth, especially we ourselves and all persons, are as a kind of vesture or sensuous Appearance : that under all these lies, as the essence of them, what he calls the ' Divine Idea of the World ; ' this is the Reality which lies at the bottom of all Appearance. To the mass of men no such Divine Idea is recognisable in the world ; they live merely, says Fichte, among the superficialities, practicalities, and shows of the world, not dreaming that there is anything divine under them."—*Hero-Worship.*

As the idea of music may exist independent of sound, yet, to be communicable, demands some voice or instrument, so all earthly things are as the tones of music, or under another figure, Vestures, making manifest to our faculties the underlying idea. So what we call rationally Society, is to the transcendentalist the embodied idea of a communion of spirits upon earth. This idea of society is a complex one; two of its principal components are Religion and Polity—and of these and their different vestures or manifestations in Church and State, our English transcendentalist principally treats.

This being the root-idea, we have said it always presents itself to him in a particular aspect, which he has expounded in his 'Sartor Resartus.' It appears to him that the last suit of clothes with which the world was invested is worn out. In Church and State, and all Society, he sees only looped and windowed raggedness. All the institutions in which the moral necessities of man are embodied, are in decay and ruin—even as the world's former wardrobes of paganism, and monkery, and chivalry, exist only in museums. The world is out at elbows, and the time is out of joint; and Mr Carlyle, not without sad appreciation of the cursed spite which dwells in the circumstance, believes that he was born to set it right.

He tells us himself that the main thing to inquire about in every man, is the significance which the idea of the world bears for him. Now we see that the idea with which Mr Carlyle's earthly habitation impresses him, is a very melancholy one — everywhere dust, rags, shabbiness, mildew, and cobwebs inhabited by monstrous spiders. The most cheerful nature once fully possessed with this imagination, and habituated to look on this scene of moral desolation, must inevitably catch a sympathetically mournful, if not dreary hue: the brightest lake overhung by such a sky must be dark and dismal.   Hence the picture conveyed to the reader, with more or less of a kind of forcible vagueness in all his works, is that of—This Planet in Tatters, and Mr Carlyle weeping over it.   Such a doctrine, " Woe to thee, O Planet! " can, if conveyed in a prophetic tone, appear only as a Jeremiad.

But there is still, we learn, a hope for the world in its mendicancy.   It may yet be extricated from Rag Fair and St Giles's, and become presentable in the best society.   Tailors capable of taking its measure and fitting it with comfortable and convenient vestments have existed ere now, and may appear again.   The great thing will be to know these master-tailors when we see them, and to distinguish them from mere pretentious snips.   Therefore Mr Carlyle, after the exposition of his Clothes- (or rather old clo')-Philosophy, sets forth his idea of who these people were in time past, so that in selecting our tailors hereafter we may be able to discriminate Stultz from Moses and Son.

In another book his idea lay still in the same direction.   He resolved to show us a better state of things in vivid contrast with their present aspect— the difference between the world in a new suit made to order, and an old threadbare one which it has out-grown ; and taking for his text an ancient chronicle then recently discovered, he preached thereon in illustration of his former doctrine.

In his 'French Revolution' he showed us how the world, with hideous ruin and combustion, had in late times set about burning some of its rags, and in so doing had nearly set the planet on fire—a measure leading on the spot to sans-culottism and great sacri-fice of decency—and to subsequent attempts to cover its nakedness with meagre classical draperies, im-perial liveries, and such integuments, in fact, as came to hand. And as there still remained to apply his doctrines to the actual existing facts and conditions of life in England, so, in a series of pamphlets, called in allusion to the period of decadence which they were discussing, "Latter-Day," he mourned like a prophetic Gibbon over the Decline and Fall of Britain.

There is this great disadvantage in setting up for a prophet and denouncer, that it forbids any measure, qualification, or moderation of utterance. A prophecy with a parenthesis—a denunciation hampered with a saving clause—would be anti-climaxes as absurd (odds pistols and triggers !) as Bob Acres's pedantic swearing, and ineffectual as a fiery warrior with a wooden leg. So that if those who expect in an his-torian the judicial calmness, and the discrimination and balance, at least seemingly impartial, to which

model historians have accustomed them, should miss
these attributes in Mr Carlyle, and are not content to
find instead the novel historical faculty of announcing an opinion or delineating a character finally and
dogmatically, in accordance with some hidden or
capricious standard, they will know how to account
for their disappointment.

But we are very far from pretending (as we shall
presently show) that there are not merits in Carlyle
to balance these faults.   And yet his very merits
render his popularity the more unaccountable.   He is
the very man, we should have said, who, in finding
fit audience, would find it also few.   The success of
a popular favourite is generally intelligible.   The
large-hearted sentimentalist who shampoos our sympathies, and the satirical detective who titillates our
antipathies, both appeal to extensive sections of the
community, for many love to snivel, and many to
sneer.   That comprehensive class of readers whose
hearts are neither very good nor very bad, delights
in the exercise of the cheap benevolence and the
harmless censoriousness which consist in weeping
over imaginary virtue in distress with the one, and
contemning fictitious baseness with the other.   To
laugh with the genial spirit who sheds a rich light
of humour over the world, gilding even its squalor—
to be absorbed in the succession of splendid pictures
of the past, which some great artist, whether as
novelist or historian, reveals—to surrender ourselves

to the musical spells of a poet, are confessions of sympathy which to most men are involuntary, and he who demurs had better for his own sake be silent. But the class of writers called of late Thinkers— those who do not take the world as they find it, and make that their subject, but who investigate its hidden moral and intellectual machinery — necessarily address a smaller audience, because they appear to exclude all whose imagination does not preserve a certain rare equilibrium with their reason. Therefore, when we are told that Carlyle is a Thinker, we are unprepared to find him a popular favourite even before we know anything further about him— when we find the style in which his thinking is done, the strangeness becomes a marvel; but when we find, as we sometimes do, that the style continues while the thinking is left out, the marvel becomes a prodigy.

We have indicated the links which, as it appears to us, unite his works into a series; but it will be desirable for the elucidation of some of his doctrines and tenets, to take a more scrutinising though still rapid survey of some of the works individually. And first 'Sartor Resartus,' which no doubt Mr Carlyle would himself indicate as containing the germ of his expansive and efflorescent (though we dare not say fruitful) philosophy.

Under the type of clothes and the various aspects they have given and give to mankind, he teaches how the institutions of society, without which man were morally naked and savage, and which are strictly speaking accidents, may, if accepted as natural and inevitable conditions of being, instead of as the mere outward investiture of those conditions, render the social man not merely a partly artificial, but a wholly unnatural existence. He teaches also that these institutions, being only the product of circumstances, and constructed for the convenience of particular needs, may, in such change of circumstances as must in the inevitable progression of human affairs occur, cease to be a shelter and defence, becoming irrelevant, cumbrous, and eventually even suffocating as a suit of chain-armour at Inkerman. Under these circumstances, what is bewildered man to do? Return to "the Divine Idea," says Mr Carlyle—place himself again in relation with "the eternal facts"—push aside the adventitious and conventional environments and stand face to face with what lies below, till he descries some means of reconciling the necessities of man in the altered time with the possibilities which the time offers. If this can be done by adapting existing institutions to present necessities, so much the better; if not, then at any cost man must not live in the perpetual falsehood of such environment, but seek deliverance and truth even in defiance and destruction.

Man, says the transcendental philosophy, is a

spirit ; but a spirit hampered with temporary earthly conditions, and manifesting itself even in its communion with other spirits only through earthly faculties to earthly senses. Who would guess Shakespeare to have been a transcendental philosopher? Yet when he tells us that

> "The cloud-capt towers, the gorgeous palaces,
> The solemn temples, the great globe itself,
> Yea, all which it inherit, shall dissolve,
> And like an unsubstantial pageant faded,
> Leave not a wrack behind ;"

and when, too, he goes on to say—

> " We are such stuff
> As dreams are made of, and our little life
> Is rounded with a sleep,"

he expresses the spirit of that philosophy. The solemn temples (all the outward forms which the spirit of religion takes); the gorgeous palaces (dwelling-places of power in one form or another); the great globe itself, or temporary theatre, wherein the spirits of men strut out their little lives before the universe with Time for the scene-shifter,—are circumstances of our dream under which the dreaming spirit seeks to accommodate itself to the conditions of dreamland. These will dissolve—out of our dream we shall each and all suddenly awake—and our awakening may be anticipated from two points of view. Either starting awe-stricken out of existence we shall be soothed like frightened children, and find that life was all a vision ending with the sleep that rounded it ; or we shall find that we have been enacting as solemn a reality as the universe contains. Mr Carlyle holds the latter belief—not as mere conviction of reason, but as ever-present faith in the fact, imbuing his life and opinions : hence he is an eminently earnest man, and to this earnestness may be traced at once the best and the worst qualities of his writings. For to stand in such close relation to the actualities of life as to be a practical man, and at the same time to let them sit so easily as to be able to detect always under them the abstract idea which they embody, is a task almost too hard for the very highest mind; and accordingly, whatever we may think of Mr Carlyle in the capacity of spirit, theorist, or thinker, we shall find him but a slipshod reformer or projector. Where a truth is to be discovered or an error exposed, who more acute ? but when you look for remedy or reconstruction, you find either silence or fantasy.

Not choosing for some reason or other to bring these doctrines before the world absolutely in person, he assumes a thin and odd disguise. He makes a kind of pretence, intentionally transparent, of having received a volume from a German friend with the peculiar name of Diogenes Teufelsdröckh, whose intervention was held necessary, we imagine, partly to break the rude shock of such novel opinions against an unsuspecting and unprepared public—

and partly to exemplify, under the German domino, the kind of life and experience which might lead a certain order of mind to originate such opinions, and follow them out in their, perhaps desperately subversive, consequences. Teufelsdröckh has the real and fanciful so mixed as to constitute the grotesque, —the real being founded, we suppose, in part at least, on Mr Carlyle's own experiences—the fanciful apparently assumed partly for the sake of indulging an odd humour, partly from a desire to invest the whole work by means of the principal figure with a certain unreality, thus leaving adverse criticism to fight the air.

Built, then, on a basis of truth, and treated thus grotesquely, the incidents of Teufelsdröckh's life are so fashioned as to favour the growth of a mind capable of conceiving and expounding his Clothes-Philosophy, which strips things of their time-wrought vestures, and looks always at the truth naked as it was born. His infancy is such as to teach him submission and meditation. Then follows an omnivorous boyhood, vigorously digesting what knowledge it devoured. So far, we have merely the substratum of a patient philosophic spirit; but now circumstances begin to decide its direction. He receives an academic education, mechanical and profitless because appealing to no higher faculty than memory. Then comes Rationalism, not merely as opposed to mysticism, but to all Idealism, picked up, he says,

along with his College studies of metaphysics, ety-
mology, and natural science, which brings him at
last to see in the Universe only a machine.   While
in this phase of his spiritual career he is trying to
begin the world, but finds no opening for him in
life — no peg on which to hang his capacity of
thought and work, although the capacity is already
recognised.

> "By degrees, those same established men, once partially in-
> clined to patronise him, seem to withdraw their countenance,
> and give him up as 'a man of genius,' against which procedure
> he, in these Papers, loudly protests.  'As if,' says he, 'the
> higher did not presuppose the lower ; as if he who can fly into
> heaven, could not also walk post if he resolved on it !  But
> the world is an old woman, and mistakes any gilt farthing for
> a gold coin ; whereby being often cheated, she will thenceforth
> trust nothing but the common copper.' "—(*Sartor*, p. 76.)

This time is a time of real misery, and discontent
is fast turning to revolt.  He has tried to form friend-
ships and failed—this machine of the universe is to
him not merely a dull and unproductive, but a hostile
and inexorable machine—all within and without is
barren and dreary, till a new epoch dawns and brings
into play his poetic faculty.

"In every well-conditioned stripling," says Teufelsdröckh, "as I conjecture, there already blooms a
certain prospective Paradise, cheered by some fairest
Eve ; nor, in the stately vistas, and flowerage, and
foliage of that Garden, is a Tree of Knowledge, beautiful and awful in the midst thereof, wanting.  Per-

haps, too, the whole is but the lovelier, if Cherubim and a Flaming Sword divide it from all footsteps of men ; and grant him, the imaginative stripling, only the view, not the entrance."

He is in love—but here too is fresh suffering for poor Teufelsdröckh—the flaming sword interposes between him and his wish.  Having given his heart with such lavish outpouring as only the poet-philosopher can, disappointment suddenly congeals it, and that fountain of feeling is closed for ever.  To escape from memory and himself, he roams over the earth, " flying with Hunger always parallel to him, and a whole infernal chase in his rear ; so that the countenance of Hunger is comparatively a friend's."

Here, then, we have Teufelsdröckh in that Valley of the Shadow which Goethe entered in company with Werter and passed through, but from which Byron never emerged.  The time had come when, finding nowhere any sympathy, his glance which had been so eagerly directed on the faces of his kind and on the world, seeking occupation for his capabilities of heart and mind, turned inward on himself, and saw only powers wasted, charities soured, and all existence marred.  At such seasons the spirit, believing itself defrauded of its rightful enjoyments, snatches in greedy discontent at whatever unsatisfying solacements offer, and thanklessly swallows them.  This is the time of revengeful opposition to

a world so ungenerous, conditions of life so insoluble
—the time of doubt and malignant questioning.
Thus we see Teufelsdröckh landed in that barren
region where the only truth discoverable for him
seems to be that whatever is is wrong.

Fortunately Teufelsdröckh, we are told, "consumed
his own choler, as some chimneys consume their own
smoke," without troubling the world with his wrath.
His unrest vented itself in nothing worse than loco-
motion.   Nature, in her various aspects, soothed his
spirit into harmony.   He begins to perceive that
there is a higher object than to be happy—that he
can do without happiness—and, with sudden strength,
he resolves to defy suffering, and conquer it, let it do
its worst.   From the solid footing of this resolution
he comes struggling out of the depths of denial into
the elevated region of calm sympathetic philosophy,
and in this state pursues to different purpose the
speculations which the old period of doubt and discontent had suggested.   Henceforth he is sorrow-
proof; "malice domestic, foreign levy, nothing can
touch him further," and looks on man and the world
with the manifold insight which he has been at different stages of his existence acquiring; the patient
thoughtfulness and wonder of childhood—the indus-
trial energy of boyhood—the reasoning powers and
questioning spirit developed in youth—the sympathy
of friendship and the poetry of love, both awakened
in manhood though unsatisfied,—these are the win-

dows through which he surveys life from the storm-proof mansion he has built for his soul. Who knows but that Byron's chafing spirit might also, had he lived longer, have chafed itself into such noble issue?

Here we have Teufelsdröckh at last fully equipped and accounted for. He has all this time been casting the outward semblances of the world into his crucible, and at length they evaporate in the continual heat of his imagination, till nothing is left except the indestructible root-idea of existence. Face to face with this residuum we might at last, after all this preparation, expect some profitable result. But we regret to say that Herr Teufelsdröckh, with his elaborate biography and spiritual career, has been called into existence to no great ultimate purpose. He does not seem to know what this residuum is, nor anything about it, except that it is wondrous, and what he would call "unspeakable," neither of which phrases affords particular satisfaction to the inquiring reader. "Can it be hidden from the edi-" tor," he says, with some glimpse of this, "that many " a British reader sits reading, quite bewildered in " head, and afflicted rather than instructed by the " present work? Yes, long ago has many a British " reader been, as now, demanding with something like " a snarl, 'Whereto does all this lead, or what use is " 'in it?'" The answer is somewhat vague and disappointing. To be told that, "if thou seest and feelest that thy daily life is girt with wonder, and based on wonder, and thy very blankets and breeches are miracles — then art thou profited beyond money's worth "—sounds as much like the facetiousness of a merry-andrew as the wisdom of a sage ; and when further informed that, "perhaps by this time thou " art made aware that all Symbols are properly " clothes ; that all Forms, whereby spirit manifests " itself to sense, whether outwardly or in the im- " agination, are Clothes ; and thus not only the " parchment Magna Charta which a tailor was nigh " cutting into measures but the Pomp and Authority " of Law, the sacredness of Majesty, and all inferior " Worships (Worth-ships) are properly a Vesture and " Raiment ; and the Thirty-nine Articles themselves " are articles of wearing apparel (for the Religious " Idea) "—the reader will still think, perhaps, that for such a result it was scarcely worth while to invoke the solemn spectre of Teufelsdröckh.

Though a metaphorical style shows great richness of mind, and is in its effect on other minds highly productive, yet it has, especially for the exposition of a creed or philosophy, its disadvantages.    It appears to us that in selecting clothes as his em- blem, Teufelsdröckh has started with a false root- metaphor, from which his sequence cannot but diverge into wider error.    To us it seems that clothes would have been a fitter emblem for the manners and customs of a nation, than for matters so essential, so life-receiving, and, in great measure, life-giving as its Institutions; matters to be no more hastily slipped off than one's skin, to the functions of which, indeed, theirs are analogous. Some perception of this Teufelsdröckh shows in his chapter on Organic Filaments, where, it appears, the old tissues are being gradually renewed—Literature being, we are told, the direction in which we are to look for a new Gospel.

That Teufelsdröckh's imputed cheerfulness of temperament has not, in his later and happier circumstances, tinged in the least his philosophy, may be discovered from the following extracts from some of his later chapters; first, this from the chapter on Church-Clothes.

"Meanwhile in our era of the World, those same Church-Clothes have gone sorrowfully out-at-elbows: nay, far worse, many of them have become mere hollow Shapes, or Masks, under which no living Figure or Spirit any longer dwells; but only spiders and unclean beetles, in horrid accumulation, drive their trade; and the mask still glares on you with its glass-eyes, in ghastly affectation of Life,—some generation and half after Religion has quite withdrawn from it, and in unnoticed nooks is weaving for herself new Vestures, wherewith to reappear, and bless us, or our sons or grandsons."

And these are his general conclusions :—

"Putting which four singular Chapters together, and along-side of them numerous hints, and even direct utterances, scattered over these Writings of his, we come upon the startling yet not quite unlooked-for conclusion, that Teufelsdröckh is one of those who consider Society, properly so called, to be as good as extinct; and that only the gregarious feelings, and old inherited habitudes, at this juncture, hold us from Dispersion, and universal national, civil, domestic, and personal war !  He says expressly : 'For the last three centuries, above all for the last three quarters of a century, that same Pericardial Nervous Tissue (as we named it) of Religion, where lies the Life-essence of Society, has been smote at and perforated, needfully and needlessly; till now it is quite rent into shreds; and Society, long pining, diabetic, consumptive, can be regarded as defunct ; for those spasmodic, galvanic sprawlings are not life; neither indeed will they endure, galvanise as you may, beyond two days.

" ' Call ye that a society,' cries he again, 'where there is no longer any Social Idea extant ; not so much as the Idea of a common Home, but only of a common over-crowded Lodging-house ?  Where each, isolated, regardless of his neighbour, turned against his neighbour, clutches what he can get, and cries " Mine ! " and calls it Peace, because, in the cut-purse and cut-throat Scramble, no steel knives, but only a far cunninger sort, can be employed ?  Where Friendship, Communion, has become an incredible tradition ; and your holiest Sacramental Supper is a smoking Tavern Dinner, with Cook for Evangelist ?  Where your Priest has no tongue but for plate-licking : and your high Guides and Governors cannot guide ; but on all hands hear it passionately proclaimed : *Laissez faire ;* Leave us alone of *your* guidance, such light is darker than darkness ; eat you your wages, and sleep ?

" ' Thus, too,' continues he, ' does an observant eye discern everywhere that saddest spectacle : The Poor perishing, like neglected, foundered Draught-Cattle, of Hunger and Overwork ; the Rich, still more wretchedly, of Idleness, Satiety, and Over-growth.  The Highest in rank, at length, without honour from the Lowest ; scarcely, with a little mouth-honour, as from tavern-waiters who expect to put it in the bill.  Once-sacred Symbols fluttering as empty Pageants, whereof men grudge even the expense ; a World becoming dismantled : in one word, the CHURCH fallen speechless, from obesity and apoplexy ; the STATE shrunken into a Police-Office, straitened to get its pay ! ' "

Certainly this is not pleasant; but the question is not, is it pleasant, but is it true? And is it? Is all England one vast dyspeptic nightmare, where the agonising struggle may at any moment end in apoplexy and death? Or is the gloom only in the mind of the seer? To him who reads merely for vivid imagery, declamation, odd denunciation, and prophetic wrath, these paragraphs are very grand and imposing. But for him who looks up from the volume and sees around him this land of England, where not only are justice, liberty, and right, secured, so far as human institutions can secure them, for all, but where a vast proportion of the inhabitants live in such comfort, plenty, and enlightened enjoyment, as was never before known, and hardly dreamt of, by the most far-seeing of past legislators; where for the rich not to practise benevolence is the contemned exception; and where, for the most part, those only who can afford it contribute to the maintenance of the vast framework of administration which shelters from injustice even the most indigent and friendless;—to such a reader, Teufelsdröckh's eloquence is merely a passionate lament that England is not Paradise, nor all its inhabitants sages and angels.

In adopting this clothes-idea of the Germans, Carlyle reminds us of the prince in the Arabian tale who vaulted without due instruction on the enchanted horse. He turns the peg, Metaphor, which lies close to his hand before the saddle, and is presently carried, not merely off the earth, but out of human knowledge. And until he shall descry and avail himself of the other peg, Fact, lying also within reach behind the ear, he will continue that balloon - like career, the course of which neither aeronaut nor spectators can control or predict.

To the ordinary readers, these few tracings of 'Sartor Resartus,' or Carlyle's Profession of Faith, may not be unacceptable : for to many a clever and even thoughtful man the book will at first have less coherence and clearness than the 'Pilgrim's Progress' has for an intelligent heathen. We have said nothing as yet about the peculiarities of style, nor of the continuous never-pausing stream of thought, with its rich freight of vivid imagery, which no one can consider without admiration and wonder. Our business lies at first with the philosophy which has given birth to all his works and opinions, which seems to us, on his own showing, so fruitless of result, but from which he augured such miraculous benefits. In his essay on Novalis, whom we may call the transcendent transcendentalist—for he seems to have got into an eighth heaven, while the others are still in the seventh—and which was published two years before the 'Sartor,' he tells us that

"The reader would widely err who supposed that this transcendental system of metaphysics was a mere intellectual card-castle, or logical hocus-pocus contrived from sheer idleness, and for sheer idleness without any bearing on the practical interests of men. On the contrary, however false or however true, it is the most serious in its purport of all philosophies propounded in these latter centuries; has been taught chiefly by men of the loftiest and most earnest character; and does bear with a direct and highly comprehensive influence on the most vital interests of men. To say nothing of the views it opens in regard to the course and management of what is called Natural Science, we cannot but perceive that its effects, for such as adopt it, on Morals and Religion, must in these days be of almost boundless importance. To take only that last and seemingly strangest doctrine, for example, concerning Time and Space, we shall find that, to the Kantist, it yields almost immediately a re-markable result of this sort. If Time and Space have no absolute existence out of our minds, it removes a stumbling-block from the very threshold of our Theology: for on this ground, when we say that the Deity is omnipresent and eternal—that with Him it is a universal Here and Now—we say nothing wonderful—nothing but that He also created Time and Space—that Time and Space are not laws of His being, but only of ours."

We shall not stop to discuss whether the transcendental doctrines possess the magical powers which Mr Carlyle thus ascribes to them. As to the novelty of the revelations about Time and Space, we imagined that not only we, but persons who existed many centuries ago, had heard something of the heavens being destined "to pass away like a scroll," and a coming proclamation "that time shall be no more," which we thought, not unnaturally, had reference to the fleeting and evanescent nature of those circumstances of our existence. Whether the habit of regarding the world and its institutions as semblances must lead infallibly to a new and beneficial state of things, or whether things would not run their course in the absence of the doctrine—whether transcendental bees would make truer hexagons or higher-flavoured honey for knowing that their queen, unless a genuine great or Heroine Bee, with a proper sense of the divine significance of saccharine and farina, would be a sham and ineptitude; or whether the bees at a busy season might not take the mystical insect who propounded the idea for a drone, put him to death with many stings, and bury him and his doctrine decently out of the way,—are speculations which we will not here enter upon, our business being not so much with the doctrines as the use he makes of them. We will rather see how he enforces his ideas in subsequent works.

The world's affairs, he says, are to be retrieved through its heroes—and these he defines to be men who habitually rest their thoughts and acts on the eternal truths, not on the evanescent appearances of things. Still that does not bring us much nearer to those eminent persons; and therefore he tells us in his Lectures on Hero-Worship, how those whom he holds to be heroes have, at different periods of the world's traditions or history, been made manifest. In the prehistoric times the hero became a divinity; mankind could see his virtues with undimmed sense, and the truths he uttered in word or deed seemed of divine origin, so that in a few generations their admiration grew into worship. Next, when the world was too advanced for this, he was still received, if not as a divinity, yet as a divinely inspired man; and Mahomet was, and is, to the believing Moslem, the prophet of God. But at last all credit in divine inspiration vanished; the world would no longer believe that a man, however wise, was the mouth-piece of a higher power. When they talked of inspiration it was in a different sense; and they called the utterer of melodious wisdom, such as Dante and Shakespeare, a poet. Luther and Knox, who battled against tyrannical ministers of a superstitious creed, are the types of the Hero-Priest. But now a new influence was beginning to assert itself in the world. Ideas uttered in achievement, in prophecy, in song, in revolt against gigantic wrong, had each had their day, and literature through innumerable channels crept over the scene. As examples of those who used literary power for true, lasting, and important ends, we have Rousseau, Johnson, Burns (though why, unless to make the theory fit, the latter should be taken out of the category of poets and put here, we cannot imagine), with a regret, from the lecturer, that his audience were not pre-pared to appreciate a still greater literary hero in Goethe. Lastly, we have the hero in his com-manding phase as absolute ruler of men. This is his rightful heritage; and for the situation none but Transcendentalists need apply. Our choice, therefore, is exceedingly limited — almost unique.

We will just pause here to note one of the little discrepancies which men of vivid imagination, with theories to get fitted, are apt to fall into. Mahomet, Mr Carlyle tells us, was a true prophet; the proof of which is that his word has endured so long. "Are we to suppose," he asks, "that it was a miserable piece of spiritual legerdemain, this which so many creatures of the Almighty have lived by and died by? I will believe most things sooner than that. One would be entirely at a loss what to think of this world at all, if quackery so grew and were sanctioned here."

But in the Latter-Day Pamphlet on Jesuitism we find something quite inconsistent with the foregoing, for it is there written that "for some two centuries the genius of mankind has been dominated by the gospel of Ignatius, perhaps the strangest, and certainly among the fatallest ever preached hitherto under the sun . . . 'a doctrine of devils!'"

However, to resume. He has told us of many heroes in time past, but he wishes us now to have a picture of a period of such virtue in England, that a hero was not only recognised, but nominated and elected to his rightful eminence. Commenting on the old chronicle of Jocelin, a monk in the Convent of St Edmundsbury in Henry II.'s time, he gives us a most interesting, graphic, and lifelike glimpse of

that far time, which he takes occasion to contrast
with this miserable present. But though as a com-
mentary it is excellent, yet the inference he draws,
and for the sake of which the book was written,
is altogether false. He shows us how the useless
old abbot of St Edmundsbury died, and the brotherhood got from the great Plantagenet a *congé d'élire*
to choose a new one. This they accordingly effected,
and, in spite of influence and intrigue, elected a
humble and obscure Brother Samson, who in his
strange high office proved himself a veritable hero.

Yet why, as Mr Carlyle industriously infers,
should this be impossible now? Set any limited
public body to choose a real governor whose will
should be indisputable, and why should it not be
done as honestly now as in the days of the Plan-
tagenets? Samson's predecessor Hugo does not
seem to have been very veraciously chosen. Or set
those men who have elected their abbot out of a
brotherhood where everybody knows everybody, to
elect, as Mr Carlyle would wish, a king out of a
nation, and how different a task will they find it!
Where shall they look? Among all the hearsays,
which shall they believe? Amid the work done
that they know of, how shall they recognise the real
doer? First catch your hero! One might imagine,
from Mr Carlyle's talk about heroes and how blind
we are to them, that those distinguished individuals
walked about with tickets on their backs which no-

body would read—that you had nothing to do, politically speaking, but rush into a crowd, pick out the
first man labelled " Hero " in transcendental characters, and fall down and worship him ; and that this
proceeding would render unnecessary all the existing machinery of Church and State.   Now, if a
whole kingdom should be in such a condition that
the national voice or its delegates could unerringly
detect the true king or ablest man, what need of
king at all ?   Here already is the most perfect of
communities—self-governing, self-developing ;  and
if any one be invested with authority more than the
others, it is only as a kind of stoker, or, at most,
engine-driver, to look out ahead, see that the wheels
are greased, and govern the stops of the perfect self-
acting machine.   But, supposing this national condition impossible, where is the Constituency to come
from ?   If the ablest man is to be elected by an
assembly of able men, who is to elect the able men ?
Or if, by some happy concurrence of chances, they
are all got together, and we have an assembly, say
of Abbot Samsons, how shall we be sure that they
will all agree in choosing the right Plantagenet,
Willelmus Conquestor, Oliver Cromwell, or other
Carlyle - right - divine, absolute sovereign ?

If Carlyle's visions were realised, everything *must*
come right ; for with him veracity means infallibility.
It is not merely that a man shall wish to see and do
the right, as many do now, whom therefore we call

right-minded, or, in Carlylese, " veracious " men, but with the wish they must also by some mysterious process acquire the power, else they are Dead-sea apes, accursed, &c. And if the majority in England or elsewhere do acquire such a power, what Willelmus Conquestor, Oliver Cromwell, or Abbot Samson, is worthy to govern such a nation—indeed, what governing does such a nation require? It is no new opinion, no revelation by Mr Carlyle, that an absolute monarchy might be the best government, if you could get the right Absolute-monarch. The idea has occurred to other philosophers, and other men not philosophers ; but they have generally also inquired of themselves by what process is he to be got?—in the solution of which (the main and only question) our seer affords no light whatever, or only such effulgence as dwells in sighs, tears, denunciation, and lamentation, amid which the only thing clear is, that as soon as the Hero-King becomes possible, he will no longer be wanted.

In the Latter-Day Pamphlets he measured, by his standard of the " Divine Idea," all the prominent political questions of the day—to which, so far as we can discover its functions, it is frequently as inapplicable as a series of solar observations would be to assist a man in finding his way about London. After one of his customary lampoons upon this unfortunate present time, he takes occasion, in his strictures on " Downing Street," to quote his old

friend William the Conqueror as an example of how
work should be done. It seems his secretaries produced in four years the "Doomsday Book," "not
wasting themselves in Parliamentary talk." "Happy
secretaries!" exclaims Mr Carlyle — "happy William!" Is this clap-trap or not? Does he see, or
does he not, that for William all the great difficulties
which beset statesmen had vanished, and in place of
a blotted scrawl, he had a clean white paper to write
his will on? It is not so difficult to plan a road if
you can run it through any man's property, no leave
asked. It is not so difficult to make laws sufficiently
veracious, and of considerable vitality, if the only
thing possible for the people you make them for is
implicit obedience.

His favourite plan is to impute an imaginary absurdity to those he is condemning, and to declaim
thereon from his vantage-ground of the eternal facts.
Thus, in the pamphlet on Model Prisons, he assumes
that the Government and people of England wished
to coddle thieves and murderers out of pure love for
them. The plan may be a mistaken one, and has
had some ridicule heaped on it by foolish advocates,
but it is an experiment founded on reason—not, as
he represents it, an absurdity founded on maudlin
sentiment. All criminals are not irreclaimable,
neither have any, except a small proportion, committed inexpiable crimes; while even of grave offenders, many have been driven to crime by unavoid-

able misery, produced, according to Mr Carlyle, by bad government. To give those a chance of reformation who may charge their crime to the account of misgovernment, as well as to try and reclaim those who seem only temporarily or impulsively to have gone astray, is, if not practically a sound doctrine, yet by no means evidently a weak or bad one. It was believed that the old system, instead of repressing crime, only bottled it up to ferment into tenfold explosiveness. The question was, shall we continue the old system of treating every criminal (to use our author's phraseology) as a scoundrel, caitiff, and devil's messenger, who must be swept out of society and out of the world to make room for a fresh batch? or shall we try to lessen crime by converting criminals. When the doctrine is expounded or exemplified by weak men, it will, like any other doctrine, acquire a false and foolish aspect; but there is nothing in the original idea to produce any of the horrors which Mr Carlyle anticipates from its realisation.

As another instance among many of his practice of riding off triumphantly on an abuse of his own creating, he asks in the pamphlet on Parliaments,—

"My friend, do you think had the united posterity of Adam voted, and since the creation done nothing but vote that three and three were seven—would this have altered the laws of Arithmetic, or put to the blush the solitary Cocker, who continued to assert privately that three and three were six? I consider not."

But the popular voice is not invoked to decide questions of fact, but questions of opinion. Granted that the end of all national effort is to get well governed, and that our electoral system is but a blundering way to do it, yet how is it to be done better? What absolutism, democracy, oligarchy, constitutional monarchy, either electoral or hereditary, universal suffrage, or convocation of notables, however sagacious, has yet, since the world began, shown how this is to be done with even approximate success? All that has been done is to try, by theory and experiment, how it may be effected, not with more of certainty, but with less of notorious blundering. How is the problem to be solved, then? Go to the eternal facts, answers Mr Carlyle. But what if the eternal facts have already given their decision in the matter? which is, that to no society of men shall any certain method of securing excellence in government be possible—that only in darkness and bewilderment, with none but will-o'-the-wisps for guides, and deceptive appearances for landmarks, shall mortals seek political infallibility. What is the use of talking of the " Divine Idea"? What has it to do with the matter? Follow the laws of the universe, says Carlyle. But the relation of man to the universe, and of man to man, are very different matters, and it is with the latter that politics concerns itself.

His manner of dealing with questions of the day

convinces us, that with rare right-mindedness, and great genius, and imagination, he has shown singular incapacity for any other function of statesmanship than the secondary one of perpetual objection and opposition. All his learning, industry, imagination, and zeal only enable him to hit a blot, and exaggerate it into a canker imminently fatal. As a philosopher, then, expounding a doctrine of general application, we think he has been immensely overrated, looming large in clouds of his own raising. As an objector, he often allows himself to be unfairly carried away by his habit of prophesying and denouncing. As a guide, he puts into our benighted hands a lantern with no candle in it. As a moralist, he is altogether unexceptionable; yet even here we find none of the originality which his admirers so largely claim for him. That to be is better than to seem—that it is good to reverence worth—that many evils exist in the world, and that if we could find out the ablest men among us, and give them due authority, many of these might be remedied—that there is an inner light or conscience to teach us right and wrong—that there is work appointed to every man which he neglects at his peril, — these are surely no new doctrines, but old as society — at any rate old as morality and philosophy — and ages before Thomas Carlyle was born they were embalmed in the proverbs of many peoples. Yet it is by reiterating such doctrines, in forms more or less fantastic, that he has achieved his great reputation.

And yet, for a man to write so much, and *always* be true to these doctrines—keeping his footing always on the virtue and necessity of genuineness, of reverence, of conscientiousness—of the immeasurable precedence which pleasure must concede to duty— is an excellent and solid basis both for a man himself and for a reputation to rest upon. For, if sermons generally, with a fair amount of eloquence, illustrated such themes, let us but consider how much more common church-going would be—how much better it would fare with the congregations—and what gratitude and applause the discourses would earn for the preachers,—and then, how can we deny what measure of fame lies in our thanks and approval to him who devotes his life to enlarging on such noble texts, which though very old are always new, to a national instead of a parish congregation? It is one thing for a man to feel conscious that these are truths, or even to be so strongly impressed with them as occasionally to inculcate them, and another thing for a man to be so imbued with their spirit that it tinges—nay, dyes deeply—all the products of his mind. What Carlyle says of Novalis may with equal truth be said of himself: " His moral " persuasions as evinced in his writings and life, " derive themselves naturally enough from the same " source. It is the morality of a man to whom the

" earth and all its glories are in truth a vapour and
" a Dream, and the Beauty of Goodness the *only*
" real possession.   Poetry, Virtue, Religion, which
" for other men have but, as it were, a traditionary
" and imagined existence, are for him the everlast-
" ing basis of the Universe."

In discussing his works, it is impossible not to
notice his singular style.   Odd as it is, we think it
may be accounted for without charging him with
affectation.   It appears to us that a writer inculcat-
ing such opinions, who says,—" I will be genuine;
I will transcribe my exact thought in the language
that most exactly pictures it, without regard either
to elegancies of style or conventional forms of expression—of anything but literal rendering of the ideas
as I see them,—true even in this to my philosophy
of dealing not with semblances but underlying ideas,"
—may, without affectation or conscious wish to
strike the attention by singularity, write in Carlyle's
manner, by simply watching and recording his
thoughts, and the states of mind which they produce
in him.   If his thoughts habitually present themselves in the concrete, there will be a large amount
of imagery and metaphor.   If he wishes to convey
in briefest space the *whole* of what presents itself to
his mind's eye, he must resort to pregnant allusive
epithets; and, to keep his thought-laden sentences
within compass, he must, in order to admit what he
thinks essential, clip off all that is not as redundancy.

As he says himself of Cromwell's style, "Superfluity,
" as if by a natural law of the case, the writer had
" to discard. Whatsoever quality can be dispensed
" with is indifferent to him." If he wants to convey
a shade of meaning for which only an approximate
word exists, and he is not satisfied with a paraphrase,
he must alter the old word or invent a new one.
Feeling strongly, he expresses those feelings, and
seeks to arouse them in the reader, not by description, but by interjection, allusion, sarcasm, or passionate appeal.

It is possible to transcribe thought literally, and
yet never pass the limits of a correct style. In fact,
the very essence of good style is to convey the
thought with the greatest nicety, combined with
the greatest vigour. There are many passages in
Carlyle's works of the finest eloquence, to which no
purist could take exception, and which yet have
evidently occurred as he has been pursuing, without intentional change of thought or expression, his
ordinary method. But this only proves that the
literal transcript of ideas, just as they present themselves, is, in some cases, the best mode of expression—in others, not. It must depend on the value
of the idea. When the subject-matter is such as to
be best conveyed by winged metaphor, and indeed
hardly admits of other vehicle—when it is of such
intrinsic solidity and worth as to bear the keen flash-
ing light of vivid illustration, not only without loss,

but with increase of truthfulness — we get either splendid prose or high poetry. But Mr Carlyle's subject-matter, though often, is not always of this high cast; and when it is not, he sinks from manner into a most abject mannerism. Take these two examples the first of his worst, the other of his best style :—

"THE NEW DOWNING STREET.

"At present, as was said, while Red Republic but clashes with foul Bureaucracy, and nations sunk in blind ignavia demand a universal-suffrage Parliament to heal their wretchedness, and wild Anarchy and Phallus-Worship struggle with Sham-Kingship and extinct or galvanised Catholicism, and in the Cave of the Winds all manner of rotten waifs and wrecks are hurled against each other,—our English interest in the controversy, however huge said controversy grow, is quite trifling. We have only in a handsome manner to say to it, 'Tumble and rage along, ye rotten waifs and wrecks; clash and collide as seems fittest to you; and smite each other into annihilation at your own good pleasure. In that huge conflict, dismal but unavoidable, we, thanks to our heroic ancestors, having got so far ahead of you, have now no interest at all. Our decided notion is, the dead ought to bury their dead in such a case; and so we have the honour to be, with distinguished consideration, your entirely devoted FLIMNAP, *Sec. Foreign Department.*'"

The other is from 'Past and Present.' The old chronicle he has been quoting from abruptly ends, the last leaves being lost :—

"The magnanimous abbot makes preparation for departure, departs, and ——. And Jocelin's Boswellian narrative, suddenly shorn through by the scissors of Destiny, *ends.* There are no words more, but a black line and leaves of blank paper.

Irremediable : the miraculous hand that held all this theatric
machinery suddenly quits hold: impenetrable Time-Curtains
rush down ; in the mind's eye all is again dark, void: with
loud dinning in the mind's ear, our real phantasmagory of St
Edmundsbury plunges into the bosom of the Twelfth Century
again, and all is over.   Monks, Abbot, Hero-worship, Government, Obedience, Cœur-de-Lion, and St Edmund's Shrine,
vanish like Mirza's Vision, and there is nothing left but a
mutilated black Ruin, amid green botanic expanses, and oxen,
sheep, and dilettanti pasturing in their places."

Those who are offended by his style should read
some of his essays — one called " Characteristics,"
for instance, and that on Boswell's Johnson,—essays
not to be surpassed either for style or thought.

But there is one habit of his which we can never
get accustomed to, and which always recurs to us in
a ridiculous light — that of keeping some of his
images constantly by him, and reproducing them as
if they were puppets in a box.   When he sits down
to write, his peaceful study is thronged by spec-
tres of the most terrific description, invoked by the
flourish of his pen.   While he is with due incanta-
tion casting the magic bullets that are to hit and
slay the Unveracities and Ineptitudes, the charmed
circle in which he works is surrounded by a horrible
panoramic phantasmagory, where all ages and nations of the world are jumbled as in a Christmas
pantomime, or rather where all the tinsel monstro-
sities of many old pantomimes are brought up,
all battered and defaced with the wear and tear of
the former season, and the whacks of facetious clown

and irreverent harlequin, and play over again their time-worn parts in a manner suggestive rather of managerial thrift than of pantomimic art. The difficulties and obstructions of life appear to him as Frost-Giants — some familiar evils figure in the singular disguise of Mud-Demons—others gibber as Dead-Sea apisms, while the background is made up of Foam-Oceans and Stygian Quagmires, and the whole scene is surrounded by an atmosphere of Silences and Sphere-Harmonies. What you thought was a simple folly, the magician tells you is an Ineptitude, and, as a charm against it, offers you an old bone from his collection of amulets; what had hitherto passed for a weak ordinary official personage, turns out to be a Phantasm - Captain; till you either end by becoming a trustful guest at this Barmecide's feast of horrors, or else cannot help looking on your entertainer as one who has the power of bringing himself into a state of *delirium tremens* without undergoing the preliminary excesses.

Shakespeare's Prince Arthur knew young gentlemen "who would be as sad as night only for wantonness." There are young gentlemen of that complexion in England still, who, as they once adopted Byronism, or the despairing-romantic, now fall into Carlylism, or the despairing-prophetic. If this way of looking at life is true, then it would be well were all the youth of England trained in it.   But what kind of men shall we rear upon such vapourish diet?   Is it desirable that the public generally, or the thinking portion of it, shall look on the material world as clothes for a central idea ; on themselves and their fellow-men as apparitions ; on difficulties as Jötuns ; on the great mass of mankind, including most of their friends and acquaintances, as Ineptitudes and Inanities ; and on the great majority of public and private proceedings as universal Stygian Quagmires?   We shall be told that this is a very disrespectful way of speaking of the fantasies of a genius ; that when the poet's eye rolls in a fine frenzy, we should stand aloof in silent reverence.   But it is one thing for the magician to be attended by an Ariel or even a Puck, and another for him to be dogged by such a witch-rabble as hunted Tam O'Shanter, or cheered old ladies with their fascinating company in the days of King James the First.

We sometimes wonder whether Mr Carlyle carries his principles into the ordinary affairs of life; whether, when he wants to descend from the upper storey of his habitation, he avails himself of the Vesture or Appearance of the stairs, or prefers to place himself in relation to the Laws of the Universe, and precipitates himself over the bannisters, confiding in the underlying fact of gravitation?   Does he read his evening paper by the light of the eternal stars?   When he leaves his haunted study, and drops his pen, does he abjure his rough magic, bury his staff in the back garden, drown his book of spells in the water-butt, hang up on a peg in the hall, along with his wizard gown, covered with weird images like a San-Benito garment, all his doleful vaticinations, and appear as a man of this world? or does he walk abroad accompanied by the spectral crew that minister to him during the terrific period of composition? If so, he must be a cheerful and convivial associate, especially desirable about a sick-bed where the doctor wishes the depressed and haply hypochondriacal patient to enjoy some exhilarating conversation. It must be extremely agreeable for a friend, conscious of possessing only an average intellect, and very little power of philosophic remark, to know that the sage with whom he is conversing regards him as a Doleful Creature, or for another who accosts him to feel that the sagacious thinker recognises in his speech nothing but "windy babble." In his most cheerful and gallant moods young ladies may perhaps rather plume themselves on appearing to him as "snow and rose-bloom maidens;" but it must be less flattering for the greater part of his intimates to enjoy his society in the certainty that he sees in them Dilettantes and Windbags, doomed to be swept away into the Inane, their congenial element, by a speedy righteous decree which he will himself have the pleasure of announcing to them; and that he is constantly looking forward to the day

when they will all be happily got rid of, together
with the majority of the human race, and make room
for a grand Wittenagemote of Abbot Samsons, Teu-
felsdröckhs, heroes, and German mystagogues, who
will, by virtue of their veracity and power of seeing
the thing that is, at once distinguish their *Can-
ning, Kon-ning,* Cunning or Able-man, and by universal acclamation, and amid grand diapasons of the
Sphere-Harmonies, elect Thomas Carlyle to rule this
fortunate planet as Chief Nebulosity or Absolute-
Nightmare.

Let any one after diligent perusal of Carlyle's
works first realise the impression of life and society
they have left on him.  There he will see depicted,
in the darkest and most lurid colours, the spectacle
of a world sinking to ruin, inhabited by nations of
men living a life of habitual hopeless baseness and
untruth, amid the tattered mockeries of governments
and religions.  Then let him clear his brain of that
image, and look abroad on England.  He will see
laws as equitably administered, government as honest
and enlightened, charities as active, and a clergy of
life as exemplary, and of religion as genuine as in
any age he can point to.  He will look on much
misery, but also on as large a proportion of happiness as has fallen to the lot of any generation.  He
will find wrong and evil receiving a publicity which,
while it renders them unduly conspicuous over
right and good, gives them also a far better chance

of being remedied. He will see daily evidence of appalling crime, and also of widespread benevolence. He will see a thriving people, whose sense is as strong as ever, their minds no less quick and energetic and far more cultivated than those of their ancestors, and who, with much self-seeking and haste to be rich, display also much conscientiousness and regard for duty. When he has considered all this, he may, perhaps, catch a glimpse of a philosopher, whose eyes are suffused with maudlin tears, surveying the scene through spectacles tinted with the hues of jaundice.

His remedial doctrines are urged with imagination, eloquence, earnestness. Their want is the fatal want of feasibility. If we are fainting with thirst, shall we listen to him who tells us in eloquent but general terms to drink, assuring us that liquid is all we want, or to him who shows us water even in the muddiest puddle? The difficulty is not to be a philosopher, but to be a practical philosopher. Grant that we may dispense with possibilities in our conclusions, and systems of philosophy may be devised as fast as the Abbé Sièyes devised constitutions. Carlyle dwells habitually in the endless mirages of the unpractical. Work, he says—choose your divinest man—see life as I see it, in truth, not in appearance—act in accordance with the eternal facts ; and on this theme he rings the changes with intense satisfaction to himself, while the reader, who asks anxiously and honestly How? waits in vain for an answer. The tale is certainly not told by an idiot; but it is full of sound and fury, and signifies—nothing.

For this reason we call this a Mirage Philosophy —a sort of inverse mirage—not where the seer, in extremely uncomfortable circumstances, has bright visions of unreal gardens and groves watered by imaginary rivulets, but where, blessed with every comfort that liberty and enlightenment can confer, he sees in the fair, broad, honest face of England only a howling wilderness.

---

## HISTORY OF FREDERICK THE GREAT.

The foregoing preamble, we hope, may afford a standpoint from whence to view, with some fair sense of appreciation, a work of Carlyle, which, seen from the ordinary level, would appear in violently disturbed perspective. Generally the later work of a well-known author may be considered on its own ground simply, without reference to previous performances. But there are many passages in this history which must be unintelligible to those who are not familiar with the doctrines and imagery shadowed forth with dusky vividness in his former

works; for, like some distinguished writers in other
walks of literature, he seems to take it for granted
that all his readers have carefully perused, and re-
ligiously remember, everything that he has pre-
viously written; and this is the case, not only with
the ideas and images, but with the phraseology.
Strange phrases, epithets, and nicknames, occur so
frequently, that a concordance, or at least a glossary,
seems necessary to render them intelligible to a
reader who has begun with the author's last work.
He is expected to be not merely a reader, but a
student; with each successive production he is supposed to start, not from its beginning, but from the
last landing-place; and for the intelligent prosecution of his career, he is required not only to equip
himself with all the author's previous conclusions,
but to encumber himself with all his crotchets and
absurdities.  For instance, we find in one of his early
papers, that on Thurtell's trial some witness said,
" he considered Thurtell a respectable man, because
he kept a gig."  This criterion has found so suitable
a place in one of the many queer corners of Carlyle's
mind as to have become part of its regular furniture.
Henceforth all respectability depending on outward
show (vesture or appearance), and therefore worthy
to be derided, is " gig - respectability."  In each
successive work the gig is the symbol of this degree
in social existence; till at last we find what some
people might call respectability in reduced circum-

stances figuring in the singular paraphrase of " gig-
manity disgigged."

But we have already indicated the links which
seem to bind our author's works into a consecutive
whole ; and therefore he may have a better plea than
most for his continual reference to personages and
passages occurring in former productions, of which
the one in hand may be considered as the legitimate
continuation.   Looking at his subject always from
the same point of view, he thus saves himself much
repetition by assuming that what has been once indicated, explained, or established, shall in future be
taken for granted.   Whether the plea will avail with
the reader must depend on his opinion of the originality of the philosophy on which he is thus required
to bestow the coherent attention due to a scientific
work ; and to some, therefore, the practice will appear
as an agreeable stimulant, to others as an egotistical
impertinence.

In no previous work is his determination to obtrude
his own personality more uncompromising than in
this History of Frederick.   His quips and cranks
and wanton wiles begin with the first page, and continue in endless succession, sometimes monotonous,
sometimes highly diversified, till the last.   But
though there still remains much to puzzle the reader,
to whom all this is new, yet we hope that what we
have already written may render many of the chief
peculiarities intelligible, and account for others suffi-

ciently to make continuity of perusal less trouble-
some.

When, therefore, after telling us that the character
of Frederick, as popularly handed down, is that of
"a royal Dick Turpin," he goes on to say: "Had
such proved on survey to be the character of Frederick, there is one British writer whose curiosity
concerning him would pretty soon have died away;"
we infer that he has selected the Prussian monarch
as his subject because he believes him to be a veritable hero, one who "had a soul open to the Divine
Significance of Life." We know at once that his
biography is to be an elaborate illustration of the
Hero as King, of whom before we have had only
sketches and studies in Cromwell and Napoleon.
Here was to be drawn, not from fancy but from the
life and at full length, the *Can-ning* or Ableman,
who combined in himself the insight, power, and will
to perceive and do the right as a ruler of a nation.
Power more absolute, associated with simplicity more
genuine and complete, is scarcely to be found in history than in the instance of the King of Prussia,
and so far he satisfies the Carlylese requisition of
being a reality and no sham. Nor is his claim to
heroism likely to be disputed. In the warrior
who, when he was routed and almost ruined by his
own rashness, not only met and defeated a fresh
foe, but turned upon the victors, and, at the moment when no choice seemed to remain for him but

submission or extinction, converted disaster into
a glorious success, no aid from transcendentalism
is needed to recognise a hero.   But the heroism lay almost altogether in his soldier-phase, and
it will be found at most stages of the biography,
where military operations are not the theme, that he
is far indeed from showing the royalty of nature
which should characterise a born king of men.

However, he is proclaimed as hero—and we know
what that means with Mr Carlyle, who invariably
turns the old constitutional maxim that the King
can do no wrong, into a philosophical fact.  As any
one who has been branded as a Python, Mud-demon,
or Phantasm-captain, is henceforth incapacitated, as
if by legal disability, from enjoying any of those
ordinary privileges of humanity which in general
induce historians to admit something of good · in
characters however bad, so when once the sign-man-
ual, "Thomas Carlyle," has been affixed to the name .
of any favoured individual, conferring on him the
dignity of Hero or rightful king of men, the immun-
ities thereby secured to him are of infinite extent.
Oliver Cromwell and Dr Johnson, William the Conqueror and Robert Burns, Mahomet and Martin
Luther, are all, by virtue of their power of seeing
the Divine Significance of Life, included in a grand
general dispensation, and their faults or crimes
either forgiven as soon as mentioned, or interpreted
into manifestations of the heroic character.   This

determination to endow all heroes with perfection, joined with caprice altogether unaccountable in selecting them, renders it impossible to predict which of the two extreme views Mr Carlyle will take of any personage, or of any act of his life, the presumption, however, always inclining to that which is most uncommon and unexpected; so that whether he would condemn Mrs Brownrig in accordance with the 'Newgate Calendar,' as the murderess of her apprentices, or extol her with the facetious poet of the 'Anti-Jacobin,' as a heroine possessed of a mind which "shaped strictest plans of discipline," no one can presume to say. Whether King Herod, Nero, Philip II., and the Duke of Alva, were Mud-demons, or "inarticulate men of genius;" whether the judicial career of Judge Jeffreys is to be pronounced "very Rhadamanthine," or an episode of devil-worship; whether the fall of the Roman Empire, or the Peninsular war, or the Indian Mutiny, were in consonance with the "Laws of the Universe," or in opposition to that mystic code, no disciple can tell us, for it is the character of his philosophy that it always requires to be interpreted and applied by the author. Under these circumstances, a practical man, puzzled in the labyrinthine wildernesses of the world, and seeking light and guidance, might prefer some homely candle which he could carry in his hand, to the fitful irradiations of that more elaborate apparatus which, like Mr

Pickwick's dark lantern, produces effects chiefly meteoric and bewildering.

The century forming the background to Frederick and his father is certainly well calculated to bring a hero into strong relief, not merely from the dearth of great men, but from the deterioration of the elements of society. Kings were no worse, not even so bad, as they had been a century before— Charles IX. and Philip II. had no more care for their people than Louis XV. or the Emperor Leopold, and were atrocious criminals besides. But in the older time faith was alive, life was earnest, the greatest privileges of man were incessantly contended for, and the precarious intervals of calm were intensely enjoyed by men who thus " tore their pleasures with rough strife, through the iron gates of life ;" whereas, in the eighteenth century all was stagnation above, while the seeds of inquiry and intelligence below were fructifying into scepticism. No great public interests were contended for, only the small private interests of monarchs — wars were bloody lawsuits about property, involving no national considerations and exciting no national enthusiasm. Thrones stood on the backs of kneeling nations, and those who sat on them looked with a listless smile at the comedy of life, with scarcely even the pretence of being amused, but with no sense of insecurity. The courts of monarchs were no longer the culminating points of a system, but had a separate system of their own.  Royal state had degenerated into idle ceremony, reverence had its prescribed gradations, courtiership had become one of the exact sciences, and etiquette was the essence of diplomacy.  To those trained in palaces, form and observance were matters of the first importance, the influence of which extended into the minutest particulars, and the domestic life of royalty was an unwholesome and oppressive slavery.

The Court of Frederick's father was modified by the peculiar temper of the monarch, by no means with a happy result.  The only person who enjoyed any immunity from irksome restraint was the King, who enforced strict observance on others, while assuming absolute licence for himself.  Thus, while we find him driving out with his cane a deputation who waited on him, lifting his foot to kick the English Ambassador at an audience, scandalising his attendants by his want of decorum at the Austrian Court, and making his violence in the palace the gossip of Berlin, yet natural feeling and parental consideration were as rigidly set aside in his family as in the most ceremonious Court in Europe.  Etiquette caused its members full annoyance, without affording them any protection.  The eldest princess was dragged from her sick-bed, when attacked by the smallpox, to attend the royal circle; and when the nature of her disease was discovered, she was shut up alone

for fear of infection, and treated with the most in-
human neglect.   In the disposal of her in marriage
all common feeling was disregarded, without even
the excuse of reasons of policy : she was alternately
bullied and cajoled, the bullying, however, immensely predominating ; and was finally got rid of by an
alliance which seems afterwards to have been regarded by the authors of it as a disgrace.   While in
disfavour, she was kept in a captivity where she
seems to have been in real danger of starvation but
for the charity of the commiserating French Pro-
testants of Berlin.   Her recreations, and those of
her brothers and sisters, were, listening to the king's
snoring as he slept after dinner, or to his homilies
when he took it in his head to preach to them, at-
tending dismal theatrical and other diversions on
compulsion, and obeying implicitly all his caprices.
Such was his addiction to the practice of caning her
and her brother Frederick, that when he was dis-
abled by the gout, his attendants used to drive him,
armed with the crutch and seated in his easy-chair,
in exciting pursuit of the offenders round his sick-
chamber, to the great solace of the royal flagellant,
who thus made himself a sort of conductor for pain
from his own great toe to the persons of his victims.
Frederick's lot was even worse than his sister's.
He was detested by his father, whose unaccountable
hatred for him began even in childhood.   Treated
with rigour where he was entitled to affection, with

neglect where anxious care was a duty, his position was not to be envied by the child of the poorest subject in Prussia. Incessantly abused and caned in public, even in the presence of kings, after he was approaching manhood, he was at length driven by this insane and intolerable harshness to attempt his escape. He was detected, seized, imprisoned— forced to witness the formal murder of one of his friends suspected of assisting his design—married to a princess whom he disliked, and would never live with—until by dint of constant wariness to avoid offending his father, and living as much as possible apart from him, he was at length tolerated, and finally, at the close of the king's life, restored to some degree of his confidence.

To depict a great king and a great warrior spring- ing from such influences as these, so as to produce a striking example of relief by contrast, would evi- dently demand no great exercise of artistic skill. And this we have no doubt Mr Carlyle would have effected, but for two circumstances which cannot be otherwise than injurious to the effect of what pro- fesses to be a history of Frederick.

The first circumstance is, that after a glimpse of the principal figures, we are called aside to observe, through three hundred pages, the antecedent his- tory of Prussia from ages of absolute obscurity and savagery. We have before remarked that conscien- tiousness is a distinguishing feature of Mr Carlyle;

and it has led him to follow this subject with labori-
ous care, and to represent it to the reader in all the
distinctness which an incessant effort to be graphic
must, with his singular power of imparting life and
motion, secure.   If distinctness were the only requi-
site, this piece of history would be perfect; but the
life imparted to the actors is both grotesque and
galvanic.   It is the sort of life which Brougham,
Peel, and Louis Napoleon would receive, if the next
century were to find them revivified from the pictures
in 'Punch.'   Each Burggraf and Kürfurst hops,
grins, and grimaces across the scene quite alive
certainly; but if he could be endowed with consciousness as well as life, he would be rather puzzled
to recognise himself under the antic disguise and
significant (or insignificant) nickname.   However,
if all the distinctness had been preserved with
higher finish and truer effect, we should still consider that the book, as a history of Frederick, would
be encumbered by this long episode of the Hohenzollerns.   It is not pretended that the events described had any peculiar influence in producing
Frederick, or that he derived from his ancestors any
of his characteristics.   The condition in which he
found his kingdom, and the events which led to it,
might with advantage have been condensed into a
single chapter.

The second circumstance is, that in all the re-
mainder of two whole volumes, Frederick's father is

the principal figure; Frederick himself occupying comparatively small space, and in that appearing as mean and insignificant, destitute of any noble feature or promise of greatness.  On Mr Carlyle's own show-ing he seems to have made too much of his hero's father.  "To us he has, as father and daily teacher, " and master of young Fritz, a continual interest; " and we must note the master's ways and the main " phenomena of the workshop, as they successively " turned up, for the sake of the notable Apprentice " serving there."  So far, however, the apprentice merely serves as an incidental appendage to the master.

The domestic character we have attributed to Frederick William is the one in which he has always appeared to the world; the impression being chiefly conveyed through the medium of the memoirs of his daughter, the Margravine of Baireuth.  Yet, that he had other and better claims to the notice of history in his character as King, let Mr Carlyle show.

" By degrees he went over, went into and through, every department of Prussian Business, in that fashion; steadily, warily, irresistibly compelling every item of it, large and little, to take that same character of perfect economy and solidity, of utility pure and simple.  Needful work is to be rigorously well done; needless work, and ineffectual or imaginary workers, to be rigorously pitched out of doors.  What a blessing on this Earth; worth purchasing almost at any price !  The money saved is something, nothing if you will : but the amount of mendacity expugned, has no one computed that ?  Mendacity not of tongue; but the far feller sort, of hand, and of heart,

and of head ; short summary of all Devil's-worship whatsoever.
Which spreads silently along, once you let it in, with full purse
or with empty ; some fools even praising it : the quiet *dry-rot*
of Nations !   To expugn such is greatly the duty of every man,
especially of every King.   Unconsciously, not thinking of
Devil's-worship, or spiritual dry-rot, but of money chiefly, and
led by Nature and the ways she has with us, it was the task of
Friedrich Wilhelm's life to bring about this beneficent result
in all departments of Prussian Business, great and little, public
and even private.   Year after year he brings it to perfection ;
pushes it unweariedly forward every day and hour.   So that
he has Prussia, at last, all a Prussia made after his own image ;
the most thrifty, hardy, rigorous and Spartan country any
modern King ever ruled over ; and himself (if he thought of
that) a King indeed.   He that models nations according to his
own image, he is a King, though his sceptre were a walking-
stick ; and properly no other is.

"Yearly he made his country richer : and this not in money
alone (which is of very uncertain value, and sometimes has no
value at all, and even less), but in frugality, diligence, punc-
tuality, veracity,—the grand fountains from which money, and
all real *values* and valours, spring for men.   To Friedrich
Wilhelm, in his rustic simplicity, money had no lack of value :
rather the reverse.   To the homespun man it was a success of
most excellent quality, and the chief symbol of success in all
kinds.   Yearly he made his own revenues, and his people's
along with them, and as the source of them, larger : and in all
states of his revenue, he had contrived to make his expendi-
ture less than it ; and yearly saved masses of coin, and 'depo-
sited them in barrels in the cellars of his Schloss,'—where they
proved very useful, one day.   Much in Friedrich Wilhelm
proved useful beyond even his expectations.   As a Nation's
*Husband* he seeks his fellow among Kings, ancient and modern.
Happy the Nation which gets such a Husband, once in the
half-thousand years.   The Nation, as foolish wives and Nations do, repines and grudges a good deal, its weak whims and
will being thwarted very often ; but it advances steadily, with
consciousness or not, in the way of well-doing ; and after long

times, the harvest of this diligent sowing becomes manifest to
the Nation and to all Nations.

"Strange as it sounds in the Republic of Letters, we are
tempted to call Friedrich Wilhelm a man of genius;—genius
fated and promoted to work in National Husbandry, not in
writing Verses or three-volume Novels.  A silent genius.  His
melodious stanza, which he cannot bear to see halt in any
syllable, is a rough fact reduced to order ; fact made to stand
firm on its feet, with the world-rocks under it, and looking
free towards all the winds and all the stars.  He goes about
suppressing platitudes, ripping off futilities, turning deceptions
inside-out.  The realm of Disorder, which is Unveracity, Unreality, what we call Chaos, has no fiercer enemy.  Honest
soul, and he seemed to himself such a stupid fellow often : no
tongue-learning at all ; little capable to give a reason for the
faith that was in him.  He cannot argue in articulate logic,
only in inarticulate bellowings, or worse.  He must *do* a thing,
leave it undemonstrated ; once done, it will itself tell what
kind of thing it is, by-and-by.  Men of genius have a hard
time, I perceive, whether born on the throne or off it, and
must expect contradictions next to unendurable,—the plurality
of blockheads being so extreme ! "

The character of such a King could evidently be
summed up in a very different verdict from the decisive one of Macaulay ; and it was of course the
duty of an historian to give all due preponderance
to the favourable side.  But when we find Mr Carlyle casting all his weight into one scale as an indig-
nant counterpoise to the former unjust state of the
balance, till censure kicks the beam, we find ourselves still far, in the opposite direction, from a just
estimate.  A ruler who did so much to elevate his
country, cannot be abruptly dismissed as brute and
tyrant.  But on the other hand, a "dumb poet,"

who makes a hell of his household, kicks ambassadors, drives his children to despair, and drinks himself into chronic delirium, is an equally anomalous character, neither does the epithet of "inarticulate man of genius" by any means satisfy the case.

But the fact is that Frederick William was predestined by Mr Carlyle for a hero, and none of his elect can sin. It is not to be supposed that a member of the chivalrous order of St Thomas can have a weak point in his character. So, when he beats and starves his son, we are simply told "the poor youth has a bad time, *and the poor father too!*" Hence arises a new dilemma for our author, in trying to get his heroic theory fitted. There are now two heroes to be maintained in heroism, the filial and the paternal, but their relationship is decidedly unheroic. The paternal hero beats the filial with his rattan—calls him frightfully disgraceful names—starves him, and keeps him short of money. The filial responds not unnaturally with fear, hatred, and suppressed revolt. Here is evidently something to be accounted for—a problem so difficult that most people would have been glad to let go one hero, leaving him to step back, at least with one leg, into the Stygian quagmire from which he had been so deftly dragged. But Mr Carlyle is of another temper, and is ready with a most astonishing device for supporting the heroic theory without abandoning his heroes.

It appears, therefore, that the paternal hero, the

sagacious ruler and wily diplomatist, is of a nature
so simple and guileless, that an astute designing
person can make him believe anything ; and if he
is instructed in a sufficiently artful manner to hate
his children, the channels of natural affection are
straightway dried up, and refilled from the sources
of cruelty and aversion.    Here, then, is a highly
ingenious solution of the difficulty by which the
designing individual who does the mischief suffers
vicariously for the unnatural conduct of the paternal
hero, and things go on, and even grow worse, without detriment to either of the heroic characters.

To this end we learn, then, that the double marriage projected between the English prince and
princess, and Wilhelmina and Frederick, was for
political reasons distasteful to the Emperor, who
despatched a crafty emissary, Seckendorf, to Berlin,
with instructions to gain the Prussian King's confidence, and then use his influence to avert the mar-
riages.    The Emperor at the same time gains over
Grumkow, Frederick William's prime minister.
These two, whom the historian forthwith designates
as "the two Black-Artists," commence their magical
practices at once ; and as the diplomatists of the
eighteenth century were never influenced by hidden
motives, and always proceeded to their aim by the
most open and public paths, the pair are never suspected by the guileless monarch to be exceptions,
and operate with such success that we are told,

" for the next seven years a figure went about, not
" doubting it was Friedrich Wilhelm ; but it was in
" reality Seckendorf-and-Grumkow much more. These
" two, conjuror and his man, both invisible, have
" caught their royal wild Bear ; got a rope round his
" muzzle ;—and so dance him about ; now terrifying,
" now exhilarating all the market by the pranks he
" plays."

A strict logician—or indeed a person of merely
plain common-sense—might here take occasion to
inquire how far it was consistent with the heroic
character to allow itself to be played upon with
such singular facility by two Black Artists, and
turned into a dancing-bear at their will ; and might
conclude that our adroit supporter of the heroic
theory had merely shifted the dilemma by "logical
hocus-pocus." Remembering, too, how it has been
written that one of the characteristics of a hero is
not to believe in "hearsays," but to see things for
himself, we might conclude that in matters so affect-
ing the relation between parent and child, this
heroic attribute might be seasonably called into
play. However, this never seems to occur to Mr
Carlyle, who expends much virtuous and well-
directed indignation on Seckendorf and Grumkow,
expressing a sanguinary regret that they were not
both " well hanged."

As an instance of how far Carlyle will go to
serve a character of which he has a lofty opinion,

we will give a passage from his summary of the career of the Great Elector, Frederick's great-grand-father :—

"Shortly after Friedrich Wilhelm, who had shone much in the battle, changed sides. An inconsistent, treacherous man ? Perhaps not, O reader; perhaps a man advancing 'in circuits,' the only way he has ; spirally, face now to east, now to west, with his own reasonable private aim sun-clear to him all the while ?

"John Casimir agreed to give up the 'Homage of Preussen' for this service; a grand prize for Friedrich Wilhelm."— (P. 349.)

That is all Mr Carlyle has to say about this pro-ceeding. We have heard of this sort of spiral heroes before—men of tortuous veracity—principally in courts of justice; but we never before heard their circuitous proceedings justified with such contemp-tuous brevity. Henceforth let anybody who has a private reasonable aim know that, provided it remain sun-clear to him, he may advance towards it by any paths he finds most convenient, even if honour, faith, and honesty should be trampled under foot. Good news this for rascaldom—not such good news, we should think, for a moral Carlylist. If this is so, why does one of his " Latter-day Pamphlets " contain such tremendous abuse of the Jesuits, who say nothing worse—"spiral" moralists advancing towards a "sun-clear aim"? These are the obli-quities which one would think must eventually destroy all confidence in Carlyle. Suppose, now,

that it had been a Phantasm Captain, instead of a
Hero, who had played the turncoat, might we not
have something to the following effect?—

"Homage of Preussen remitted!—a great prize
*temporarily* for Friedrich Wilhelm—of considerable
value as an offset against Losses, pecuniary or ter-
ritorial, but of quite infinite *no*-value as an offset
against a Human Soul.  To do homage for Preussen,
bend the Great-Electoral knee, render public acknow-
ledgment of inferiority, is galling to a Great-Elector
—thing by all means to be abolished, if the Laws of
this Universe permit.  But to bend a Great-Electoral
knee to Beelzebub—to say to him, 'Henceforth I am
*thy* Feudatory, not John Casimir's'—this, methinks,
the laws of this Universe will by no means permit,
but will surely avenge such Transfer of Homage on
thee and Preussen," &c., &c., &c.  We will pay Mr
Carlyle the compliment to say that these sentiments,
as more respectable, are more characteristic of him
than his own.

In another place we are told that Frederick's
father, looking into the accounts of a domain, found
the books of a functionary called Hesse in confusion,
and several thousands short:—

"What has become of these thousands, Sir?  Poor old Hesse
could not tell: 'God is my witness, no penny of them ever
stuck to me,' asseverated poor old Hesse; 'but where they
are—?  My account-books are in such a state;—alas, and my
poor old memory is not what it was!'  They brought him to
Berlin; in the end they actually hanged the poor old soul;—

and then afterwards in his dusty lumber-rooms, hidden in pots, stuffed into this nook and that, most or all of the money was found. Date and document exist for all these cases, though Mr. Dryasdust gives none ; and the cases are indubitable ; very rhadamanthine indeed. The soft quality of mercy,—ah yes, it is beautiful and blessed, when permissible (though thrice accursed, when not): but it is on the hard quality of justice, first of all, that empires are built up, and beneficent and lasting things become achievable to mankind, in this world !—"

So that, when a hero hangs an innocent man, that is justice ; and when he finds it permissible to pardon an innocent man, that is mercy. This is the kind of heroism which, by a strange perversity, mankind has, in all ages, incessantly struggled to be rid of. "Very rhadamanthine indeed," is Mr Carlyle's comment—wherein he libels Rhadamanthus.

The Double-Marriage Project occupies a large space—as futile and trumpery an intrigue as ever a court was engaged in. And Mr Carlyle tells us that such is also his opinion, but he considers that he and his readers are bound, at any cost, to follow the aspirings and disappointments of family interest in all their miserable particulars, because, as he says, "there is an important young Friedrich inextricably wrapt up in it." Why "inextricably," we do not see. Actively he had nothing whatever to do with it, being a mere puppet in the hands of his father. Seckendorf, we are told, was despatched to Berlin to stop the double marriage, and Seckendorf is one of the "Black Artists" who caused or widened the breach between father and son. Could not all this be made clear without entering into every particular of the tedious double marriage? "Without a Friedrich," says our historian, "the affair could be reduced to something like its real size, and recorded in a few pages." Still more ought this to have been done with, than without, a Friedrich, whose personal history, with which we are principally concerned, it encumbers rather than illuminates.

The rest of the earlier volumes are taken up with the "Kaiser's Spectre-Hunt," or efforts of the Emperor of Austria to get the Spanish crown—the desertion and imprisonment of the crown-prince—and the rest of the acts of Friedrich Wilhelm's life, such of them as he performed when he was either drunk or delirious being described with great pathos. The labour necessary to bring full particulars to light has been endured honestly, and we wish we could add uncomplainingly; but fifty times are we called upon to appreciate and sympathise with him in his explorations, and struggles with his Incubus-foe Dryasdust —whining entreaties to pity the sorrows of a poor historian, which are not always productive of sympathy.

The labour of investigation is equalled by that of reproduction. Everywhere there is evidence of incessant care to represent people and events in the most vivid manner—and those who are familiar with Mr Carlyle's faculty of conveying shades of meaning will know what the incessant exercise of it will amount to in a long history. And here occurs again the question of style—at which we seem to hear from all his admirers loud protests. His style is to them sacred —not appreciated, because of its excellence—"caviare to the general." It aim is to reproduce with the greatest exactness all the thoughts and all the moods of mind which the contemplation of his subject produced in the author—a curious psychological study, more interesting and valuable perhaps in a History of Thomas Carlyle than a History of Frederick the Great. We have already observed that the propriety of this method of literal transcript of idea must depend on the value of the idea. But the course of a long history, which professes to deal much with common and familiar matters, and to give even to important subjects an everyday look, can afford but few fitting opportunities for its employment. It seems to us that nothing but an all-pervading self - importance could lead a man to suppose that all the operations of his mind in any direction are worthy of being carefully recorded. Other writers have been famed for their curious felicity of style, but it has been displayed with widely different effect—concealing their muscles under a most delicate and healthy skin, while Carlyle loves to exhibit his in all their bare repulsiveness. Are all the pains which such men as Hume and Gibbon have taken to secure grace as well as power, thrown away? or is there no merit in careful constructive art, as must be the case, if Carlyle is right? To see clearly and imitate exactly are only the groundwork of an artist's merit—he must be able skilfully to select, combine, and harmonise—else Titian was a bungler, and the decorators of Chinese pagodas are truer artists.

There is one distinguishing feature of Carlyle's style which renders the popularity it has attained especially curious. It is probably the most arrogant style that anybody who did not profess to believe himself inspired ever assumed. The author seems to look down on us as if from some skyey eminence—much as Jove, from his throne, may have looked down on mortal doings by the banks of the Scamander, sometimes in wrath, sometimes in contemptuous compassion. One might suppose, from his invariable tone, that the only veracious, the only sincere, the only clear-sighted individual, who surveyed this terrestrial scene, was Thomas Carlyle; that no one else had a conscience, knew good from bad, was able to exert himself to any purpose whatever, or had the smallest sense of "the Divine Significance of Life." The human race is adrift in a fog, above which he sits serene, and marks their futile efforts to blunder through, with a grim smile for some, a condescending pity for others, while for general guidance and encouragement, he exclaims with Puck, "Lord, what fools these mortals be!" Even his favourite heroes he

patronises as if they were good little boys—patting
them on the back, pinching their ears, and calling
them nicknames as Cromwell and Napoleon did with
their generals.  But let the sage take comfort—let
him be assured that he is not the sole excellence
hitherto produced, or producible, by this despicable
nineteenth century.  Other men have appeared, and
will appear in it, sounder in philosophy, clearer of
vision, as original in genius, of no less pure, though
less uproarious rectitude, and of more commendable
modesty than himself.  People who know nothing of
Fichte or his " Sensuous Appearances " have led and
will lead very good lives, and do their duty in this
world—and some day admiring readers will get tired
of Carlyle's oppressive virtue, and begin to inquire
what singular hap had befallen him that he should be
so contemptuous and impatient of his brother insects.

We do not care anything about the dignity of
history compared with its truth, nor do we insist
that an historian shall convey his narrative through
a colourless medium ; but we do insist that the
medium shall not be distorting.  We have shown
how the bent of Carlyle's philosophy brings him to
view the world's business, and the proceedings and
prospects of his fellow-creatures, in a dismal and
desponding light.  Hence the cast of his mind is
sardonic, and the style, the exact reflex of his own
mind, is sardonic too.  Everybody and everything
dealt with in his history is treated in a jeering tone

E

—the tone of a virtuous Mephistopheles. Characters enter, grimace, perform their allotted movements in an exaggerated fashion, as if their wires were pulled a little too hard—are baptised with a facetious nickname—labelled Sham or Reality—mostly Sham—and are then dismissed, as Sam Weller dismissed the Fat Boy, "with a harmless but ceremonious kick." Distinctness must be secured at any price—by a trick, if not by other means. Thus the Emperor Leopold is always, during the history of many years, "the little Kaiser in the red stockings;"—and is scarcely ever mentioned without the scarlet integuments. And why? Because, it seems, a Mr Savage, whom nobody knows anything about, describing in a book his residence at Vienna, says he saw the Emperor there, who was a little man with red stockings. Therefore, as emperors never have more than one pair of stockings, the colour of which is an infallible index to their imperial character, he is henceforth the "little Kaiser in the red stockings." The King of Prussia is always "Majesty," without any prefix, as if Majesty were his Christian name; and the King of Poland, having given unusual proofs of bodily vigour, is "the Physically Strong." These all play considerable parts in the drama, but characters that only appear to vanish are similarly treated. Thus, for instance, a former Elector of Brandenburg, three hundred years ago, had a sister who had a husband called Christian :—

"His wife was a Danish Princess, Sister of poor Christian II., King of that Country : dissolute Christian, who took-up with a huxter-woman's daughter,—'mother sold gingerbread,' it would appear, 'at Bergen in Norway,' where Christian was Viceroy ; Christian made acceptable love to the daughter '*Divike* (Dovekin, *Columbina*),' as he called her. Nay he made the gingerbread mother a kind of prime-minister, said the angry public, justly scandalised at this of the 'Dovekin.' He was married, meanwhile, to Karl V.'s own Sister ; but continued that other connection. He had rash notions, now for the Reformation, now against it, when he got to be King ; a very rash, unwise, explosive man."

The Bohemian Zisca appears to Mr Carlyle as a "human rhinoceros driven mad"—henceforth he is "Rhinoceros Zisca." Waldemar, a Markgrave, died, and a false Waldemar, pretending to be him, afterwards appeared—he is "*post-mortem* Waldemar," or "*post-obit* Waldemar."

Events are treated in the same grotesque fashion. The Emperor wishes the maritime powers to join him against France :—

"The astonished Kaiser rushes forward to fling himself into the arms of the Sea-Powers, his one resource left : 'Help ! Moneys, subsidies, ye Sea-Powers !' But the Sea-Powers stand obtuse, arms not open at all, hands buttoning their pockets : 'Sorry we cannot, your Imperial Majesty. Fleury engages not to touch the Netherlands, the Barrier Treaty ; Polish Elections are not our concern !' and callously decline. The Kaiser's astonishment is extreme ; his big heart swelling even with a martyr-feeling ; and he passionately appeals : 'Ungrateful, blind Sea-Powers ! No money to fight France, say you ? Are the Laws of Nature fallen void ?' Imperial astonishment, sublime martyr-feeling, passionate appeals to the Laws of Nature, avail nothing with the blind Sea-Powers : 'No money in us,' answer they : 'we will help you to negotiate.' 'Negotiate!' answers he ; and will have to pay his own election broken-glass, with a sublime martyr-feeling, without money from the Sea-Powers."

If this is fine history, we should think Mrs Gamp would have made a fine historian.

Why should a person wishing to learn something of Frederick's history be treated to a passage of this kind ?—

"Would the reader wish to look into this Nosti-Grumkow Correspondence at all? I advise him, not. Good part of it still lies in the Paper-Office here, likely to be published by the Prussian Dryasdust in coming time ; but a more sordid mass of eavesdroppings, kitchen-ashes, and floor-sweepings, collected and interchanged by a pair of treacherous Flunkeys (big bullying Flunkey and little trembling cringing one, Grumkow, and Reichenbach), was never got together out of a gentleman's household. To no idlest reader armed even with barnacles, and holding mouth and nose, can the stirring up of such a dustbin be long tolerable. But the amazing problem was this Editor's, doomed to spell the Event into clearness if he could, and put dates, physiognomy, and outline to it, by help of such Flunkey-Sanscrit !—That Nosti-Grumkow Correspondence, as we now have it in the Paper-Office,—interpretable only by acres of British Despatches, by incondite, dateless, helpless Prussian Books ('printed Blotches of Human stupor,' as Smellfungus calls them): how gladly would one return them all to St Mary Axe, there to lie through Eternity ! It is like holding dialogue with a Rookery ; asking your way (perhaps in flight for life, as was partly my own case) by colloquy with successive or even simultaneous Rookeries. Reader, have you tried such a thing ? An adventure never to be spoken of again, when once done !"

It is heartily to be wished that these earlier volumes had contained more of solid merit as a set-off against such passages as these.   But the truth is, that with a strong wish to discover historical excellence in this memoir of an eminent king and soldier, we have been driven to the reluctant con-clusion that in no previous production of Carlyle's has the halfpenny worth of bread borne so small a proportion to the intolerable deal of sack.   For-merly we took his guineas, notwithstanding the fan-tastic image and superscription, for the sake of the genuine gold.   But when he takes to giving us gilt farthings of the same pattern—excuse us, sir,—think of the police and the laws against counterfeit coin.

This painful circumstance of writers abandoning their strong points and carefully cultivating their weak ones, we always attribute to the influence of indiscreet foolish admirers.   O those admirers, how they ruin our distinguished men !   They seize on a peculiarity, and laud it as if it were the essence of the man—they tell him an accidental wart is his most expressive feature—till he actually grows proud of his wart, and parades it instead of decently hiding it with sticking-plaster, or at any rate ignoring it.   We figure to ourselves our historian, pen in hand, wear-ing a saturnine smile which broadens into a sardonic grin as he jots down an extraordinary prank of lan-guage which will astonish Moddle, or a verbal antic which he rather thinks will amuse Noddle—taking

Moddle and Noddle for the critical world.    Here a
a few of the gilt farthings we speak of :—

" He that was honest with his existence has always meani
for us, be he king or peasant.   He that merely shammed a
grimaced with it, however much, and with whatever noise a
trumpet-blowing, he may have cooked and eaten in this worl
cannot long have any.   Some men do *cook* enormously (let
call it *cooking*, what a man does in obedience to his *hung*
merely, to his desires and passions merely),—roasting who
continents and populations, in the flames of war or other d
cord;—witness the Napoleon above spoken of.   For the app
tite of man in that respect is unlimited ; in truth, infinite ; a
the smallest of us could eat the entire Solar System, had
the chance given, and then cry, like Alexander of Macedo
because we had no more Solar Systems to cook and eat.   It
not the extent of the man's cookery that can much attach
to him ; but only the man himself, and what of strength he h
to wrestle with the mud-elements, and what of victory he g
for his own benefit and mine."

" Capital !" says Moddle.   " Highly suggestive
says Noddle.   " Trash !" says the irritated gener
reader.

Another farthing—

" But the Fates appointed otherwise ; we have a
to accept our Fate !"

Another—

" All things end, and nothing ceases changing ti
it end."   This is a double imposture—it is not eve
an original sham, coming as it does from the wel
known mint of Mrs Gamp, " Vich likeways is tl
hend of all."

Here is a very magnificently gilded farthing—

"Just about threescore and ten years ago, his speakings and his workings came to finis in this World of Time; and he vanished from all eyes into other worlds, leaving much inquiry about him in the minds of men." The plain copper is that Frederick died—the gilding, therefore, is rather thick.

But it is at the most interesting point of this narrative that he gives us what may be considered the climax of his profound reflections. The King has imprisoned his son, and thinks of putting him to death—and our chronicler, winding up his chapter impressively, remarks, "*Here has a business fallen out, such as seldom occurred before!*"

Formerly his images, however absurd, always preserved a consistency which rendered their effect decisive. Now we frequently have the absurdity without the consistency. Frederick, we are told, is "a man of infinite mark," whatever distinction that may imply. He also, we are told, has a "snuffy nose rather flung into the air, under its old cocked-hat—like a snuffy old lion on the watch." A lion in a cocked-hat, and addicted to snuff, gives a new impression of the animal; but he subsequently figures still more strangely as a vocalist. "Friedrich Wilhelm's words, in high clangorous metallic plangency, and *the pathos of a lion raised by anger into song*, fall hotter and hotter." This may have been suggested by some recollection of Bottom acting the lion—"I will roar you gently as any nightingale." The "high clangorous metallic plangency," however, is undoubtedly original.

It is said that Carlyle's style is easily imitated. Not certainly his best style; for to imitate that, a man must have an equal gift of imagination. But the style we have been commenting on is not difficult. Our friend Herr Botherwig (an Anglicised German, brought up from his cradle upon mystical and transcendental food) imitates it passably. Take this excerpt from Botherwig :—

"Thomas, knowing well that greedy Cormorant-Public is apt to take what grains of wheat are offered to it thanklessly, and with small thought or care for the labour of the winnower, does, with frequent iteration (lest said public should think that writing history were task light and blithesome as going a-Maying), bewail piteously, and not without lachrymose Sufflication, the painful obscuration of his philosophic spirit, while wallowing amid the inane ponderosities of the Muddemons or Prussian chronicle-writers, where is to be found much of the raw material of our Prussian-Jargonic-History. Wherefore, in revenge, Thomas calls them hard names, of which Prussian Dryasdust is the chief opprobrious epithet— name mysterious haply to Cormorant-Public, but explainable thus :—Northern-magician Scott (magician conceivably akin some way, or shall we say by left-handed relationship, to the Sphere-Harmonies), did, in sportive preamble to certain fictitious narrative, introduce supposititious antiquarian friend, under the name of Doctor Dryasdust—which cognomen, tickling the capricious Midriff of Thomas, does for him ever after officiate as Generic appellation for all of that brotherhood; and Dryasdust is forthwith stereotyped and enrolled in that singular Lexicography (not perusable by living man without wonder), along with the Pythons, Veracities, Foam-Oceans, and other Indigestions and Dire Chimæras. Whence arises

also this other question—Is there not, in the masses of Historical rubbish, some quality worse than bewildering?—is there
not, moreover, something *contagious!*"

Botherwig agitates this further question, "Whether,
in the composition of Thomas, there be not, haply,
as much of prig as genius? whether we have not
unconscious charlatanism mixed with *not*-unconscious
veracity.    What," exclaims Botherwig, "what if
thou, the sworn foe of shams, have deserted to the
Enemy!    What if thou, the Denouncer of Windbags, are also thyself a Professor of Flatulence!    O
heavens!"—Enough of Botherwig, who certainly
could not, with anything like equal success, attempt to imitate those inferior writers, Clarendon
and Gibbon.

Far, however, from becoming more and more hazy
and unintelligible as he grows older, the historian
exhibits in the later volumes fewer crotchets and
fewer freaks of style, but not less of that descriptive
and allusive power and wealth of imagery which
have always formed his chief attractions.    The "gilt
farthings" which we spoke of, the bits of commonplace palmed upon us under a thick disguise of
staring metaphor and allusion, have been mostly
withdrawn from circulation, and replaced by a more
legitimate coinage.    No doubt this view of the later
volumes is partly due to our familiarity with Carlylese, rendering us indifferent to verbal pranks, and
more sensitive to excellences.    But it is owing in

much greater degree to the improvement in his subject. He is no longer encumbered with Frederick-William, the eccentric hero of the earlier volumes, the crazy, brutal father of the soldier-king. The insupportable tediousness of such dim transactions as "Double-Marriage Projects" and "Tobacco Parliaments" (or orgies in which the crack-brained potentate indulged, along with a few congenial lunatics and idiots), happily came to an end along with their author. Frederick's boyhood, too, so squalid, so barren of interest and incident, giving so little promise or suggestion of the future conqueror and statesman, had ended before his father's death; and with the wars for which he gave the signal by the seizure of Silesia, he stands forth surrounded by figures so spirited and so martial, in the midst of such a clangour of arms and shock of nations, as would lend interest to a narrative far less picturesque in treatment and clear in effect than Mr Carlyle's. For, the same industry which formerly led the historian to grope and sift thoroughly, though with many lamentations and protests, amid the chronicles of the voluminous Dryasdusts of Prussia, and pick such scraps as suited him from the chaos of stupidity, has also induced him, as the chronicler of a conspicuous era in war, to study military problems to unusually good purpose. A man who can in a science so eminently practical, and which has for the most part been so pedantically treated, as the

science of war, discard the pedantry, arrive at common-sense conclusions, and describe military operations with unusual spirit and lucidity, must possess
faculties of whose existence there was little evidence
in his former works. Exuberance of imagery, fertility of allusion, occasional passages of vigorous eloquence in painting a scene or a character—these we
should expect from the author of ' Sartor Resartus '
and ' Hero-Worship,' but *not* a plain account of the
manœuvres of hostile armies.

It must always remain somewhat unaccountable
why a writer of Mr Carlyle's peculiar fashion and
modes of thought should have selected the history of
Frederick for a theme. It is true that he is a successful representative of that government of force which
the philosopher has always held up as the perfection
of a political system—successful, because of a small
kingdom he mâde a great power; because, with
inadequate means, he did the work and achieved the
results due to great means; because he made for
his army, his country, and himself, a fine and lasting
reputation. The power inherited from his father
suffered no diminution of absolutism in Frederick's
hands; and we should not have been surprised had
he been selected for glorification in an additional
chapter on ' Hero-Worship.' But here the work of
years is devoted to the career of a man whose great
merit was, that he was a successful fighter of battles.
A character less elevated, less fertile of opportunities

for indulging a romantic or poetic vein in the biographer, is scarcely to be found in the high places
of history.   The fact that the King, among his as-
pirations, aimed at being a poet, tells altogether
against him ; for his aim was mere versification and
Sternholdian grandiloquence, and in that he failed.
Mr Carlyle, with all his tendencies setting towards
the romantic and picturesque sides of human character — large dealings, far-reaching influence, and
high, if "inarticulate," genius, tied himself for years
to a subject which, except in the military phase, is
commonplace—crafty, unusually deficient in great
qualities or great motives, and which no amount of
gloss or drapery can present as heroic.   " Frederick's
ideal," says his biographer, " compared to that of
some, was low; his existence, a hard and barren,
though a genuine one, and only worth much memory
in the absence of better."   Why not have sought
better, then ?   It cannot, surely, be meant that none
better are to be found.

Frederick was twenty-eight years old when he
began to reign.   He had grown up amid influences
the most unfortunate and unfavourable.   The character of the personage who ruled in the home of his
youth has been already described.   None of the
ruffians who are charged before police magistrates
with brutal outrages on the members of their
wretched households could exceed in reckless and
capricious cruelty this truculent monarch.   It was

to be expected that Frederick, his intellect and sympathies alike cramped by this iron rule of savagery, would seize not the best but the readiest consolations that might offer, and that the character of his mind would deteriorate. Except in fairy tales and didactic novels, it is rare to find squalor, hardship, and oppression favourable to the development of virtue and of nobility of character. Nor did they prove so in this instance. The duplicity which habitual terror had produced in the boy reappeared in the king, but in the more respectable form of reticent statecraft. The external casing of indifference, necessary for any one who would live at all under such conditions, had become in the man a bright hard shell, impervious alike to the touch of sympathy or the blow of fate. The highest heaven he could look forward to in youth was deliverance from domestic tyranny—that attained, he saw nothing beyond either to fear or to hope for. Irreverent, practical, shrewd, brave, self-reliant, severe but not cruel, of quick decision, exacting much and rewarding sparingly or grudgingly—such was the king and leader who now stepped on the world's stage.

The stage was, at this juncture, well suited to the hero. A succession of absolute sovereigns since the feudal period had at length culminated in an order of beings who looked on the territories they ruled as their private property, to be sold, transferred, exchanged, or bequeathed, as the family

interests of the proprietor might dictate.  As might
have been expected under such circumstances,
there were, for whole districts in Europe, numerous
claimants, whether on the score of relationship to a
former proprietor, purchase, convenience, or political
exigency.    It was not difficult, therefore, for an
ambitious sovereign to find both a colourable pretext for war, and powerful allies in those who,
having similar claims elsewhere, bargained for re-
ciprocal support.   And if the times were favourable
to the picking of a quarrel, they were no less so to
its prosecution, by a sovereign of exceptional ability.
For at this time there were in Europe no great
leaders, either in politics or war.   Dull or frivolous
sovereigns occupied the thrones, and suffered favour-
ites or mere routine statesmen to dictate their
policy.   The great generals of a preceding generation, Turenne, Marlborough, Eugene, had left repre-
sentatives only of their system of war, not of their
genius.   Pedantry—that is to say, an extreme addiction to forms, without reference to their meaning
or their applicability—was the characteristic in the
training of armies and the conduct of generals, and
ruled as absolutely in the field as other forms of
incapacity in council.   Contests, begun for petty
and private objects, grew in their progress aimless
and unmeaning, and chicanery had become, in an
unusual degree, an element of statecraft.

On such a scene, amid such competitors, Frederick was peculiarly fitted to succeed.  A man of high and noble character—a Bayard or a Turenne—would have entered the field with obsolete armour and weapons.  But Frederick was as remarkable for astuteness as for vigour; and amid the shifting politics of the time, he had the advantage of a clear and definite object.  His design was to seize, at the first favourable opportunity, the Austrian province of Silesia; and either to retain it, or make of the possession of it a lever by which to wrest from Austria a recognition to his title to certain territories on the Rhine; and the necessary, or at any rate judicious, preliminary to such seizure must be the establishment of a fair-seeming pretext.

Silesia had never been Prussian.  But more than two hundred years before Frederick's time, his ancestor, the Elector of Brandenburg, had made a compact with the Duke of Liegnitz, lord of considerable territories in Silesia, by which either prince, on failure of heirs to the other, was to succeed to their joint dominions.  As the Duke was a vassal of the King of Bohemia, the monarch's sanction had been necessary to render the arrangement valid.  But this king's successor, fearing perhaps to see a too powerful neighbour established on his borders, had recalled the sanction, and the deed had been cancelled by state authority; the vassal had been compelled to give up his parchments, but the Elector of Brandenburg had refused to part with his.

In 1675, a hundred and forty years afterwards, the
last Duke of Liegnitz died, and the Elector of Brandenburg, reviving the old question, urged his claim
upon the Emperor Leopold. Let Mr Carlyle describe the colloquy :—

"Kaiser Leopold in the scarlet stockings will not hear of
Heritage-Fraternity. 'Nonsense!' answers Kaiser Leopold:
'a thing suppressed at once, ages ago ; by Imperial power :
flat *zero* of a thing, at this time ; and you, I again bid you,
return me your papers upon it.' This latter act of duty Fried-
rich-Wilhelm would not do ; but continued insisting. 'Jagerndorf at least, O Kaiser of the world,' said he ; 'Jagerndorf,
there is no colour for your keeping that !' To which the
Kaiser again answers, 'Nonsense!'—and even falls upon
astonishing schemes about it, as we shall see ; but gives nothing."

Such was the claim to the duchies of Lower Silesia—founded upon a deed contracted two hundred
years before, which never took effect, and which
was formally annulled by the same authority as had
sanctioned it. The claim to Jagerndorf, a duchy in
Southern Silesia, rested on different grounds. The
younger sons of the Electors of Brandenburg had
occasionally been provided for by giving them the
territories of Baireuth and Anspach. In this way
members of a younger branch of the Hohenzollerns
appear in history as princes ; and one of these,
George, Margrave of Anspach, acquired, in exchange
for other territories which he had purchased with
his own money, the duchy of Jagerndorf. "Here-

by," says Mr Carlyle, "has Jagerndorf joined itself to the Brandenburg territories." Rather an audacious assertion, the reader will probably think, considering that the said Margrave George never ruled in Brandenburg.

The descendant of this Margrave dying without children in 1603, his duchy of Jagerndorf fell to the Elector of Brandenburg, who settled it on his second son, Johann George. This prince, joining the King of Bohemia in war against the Kaiser, was put under the ban of the empire, and his territory forfeited. On what the subsequent claim of Brandenburg to Jagerndorf was exactly founded, Mr Carlyle does not tell us; but the Electors may be presumed to have argued that the territory which they had divided from the Electorate ought to have been restored to it. But before the reader is in a position to estimate the justice of the claim, it is necessary that he should know what an advocate might have to say on the Austrian side of these questions; and as the Silesian wars are so important in the history of Frederick, the first volume of the work would have been better employed in giving us full means of forming a judgment than in the tedious and unnecessary account of Frederick's ancestors and their doings. On the evidence vouchsafed to us we should confidently say, that if such claims were to be in all cases supported by war, there could be no peace for any nation on the face of the earth.

F

From the promptitude with which Frederick acted
when the opportunity came, it is evident that he
had made up his mind about the seizure of Silesia as
soon as he became king.   Of the merits and validity
of the pretexts for the act, the reader must judge
from the summary we have just given.   For him
and for Prussia it was the most (indeed the only)
momentous act of his reign ; for his whole history is
the history of his struggle for the retention of this
Austrian province.   Of his motives the King says
himself, after recapitulating certain considerations—
"Add to these reasons an army ready for acting,
funds, supplies all found, and perhaps the desire of
making one's self a name ; all this was cause of the
war which the King now entered upon."   Perhaps
the reader will think with us that there is little
evidence here except of "low ambition and the pride
of kings."   But Mr Carlyle is of another mind about
his hero.   "This young king," he says, "is magnanimous ; not much to be called ambitious, or not in
the vulgar sense almost at all—strange as it may
sound to readers."   And on what the King himself
said about his motives he discourses as follows :— .

" 'Desire to make himself a name ! how shocking!' exclaim
several historians.   'Candour of confession that he may have
had some such desire ; how honest !" is what they do not exclaim.   As to the justice of his Silesian claims, or even to his
own belief about their justice, Frederick affords not the least
light which can be new to readers here.   He speaks, when
business requires it, of 'those known rights' of his, and with

the air of a man who expects to be believed on his word ; but
it is cursorily, and in the business way only ; and there is not
here or elsewhere the least pleading : a man, you would say,
considerably indifferent to our belief on that head ; his eye set
on the practical merely. 'Just Rights ! what are rights, never
so just, which you cannot make valid ?  The world is full of
such.  If you have rights and can assert them into facts, do
it ; that is worth doing !'"

Was ever such pleading heard out of the Old Bailey
as this of our moral historian, our guide, philosopher,
and friend?  Is it not exactly the simple code of
law of Rob Roy—

> " That he should take who has the power,
> And he should keep who can " ?

and was Rob's code " in accordance with the laws of
this universe," or was it " Devil-worship " ?

Frederick, then, being provided with a pretext,
such as it was, still wanted an opportunity.  It
came far more speedily than could have been anticipated.  Within a year of the King's accession, the
Emperor Leopold died very unexpectedly.  By the
law of the Austrian States females could not succeed, and he had daughters only.  All his life, therefore, he had been employed in impressing on the
political world (that is to say, the various Courts of
Europe) the necessity of upholding a private arrangement of his called, like similar arbitrary and
exceptional acts, "a pragmatic sanction," whereby
he decreed that his female children *should* succeed
him in the Austrian States ; and to this instrument

he had obtained the concurrence of several European powers. At his death his daughter, Maria-Theresa, became Archduchess of Austria and Queen of Hungary and Bohemia; and in the accession of this young woman, inexperienced in rule, holding her position by a questionable title, and having but a bankrupt exchequer, Frederick saw his opportunity.

Now we are not going to insist that magnanimity, or generosity, or any other large-hearted quality, ought to be the prime element in politics. On the contrary, seeing what are the mischievous results of sentimental statesmanship in our times, we rather insist that, of all motives of state policy, those which are romantic are the most pernicious. The dullest of matter-of-fact men would be much safer as a political leader than Don Quixote. Frederick's own ideas on the subject have been plainly enunciated. "My Lord," he says to the English ambassador, "don't talk to me of magnanimity; a prince" (acting not for himself but for his nation, interpolates Mr Carlyle) "ought to consult his interest in the first place. I am not against peace, but I expect to have four duchies given me." We thus far agree with the King that business is business; and a nation can no more grow great by sacrificing its interests, than a merchant can grow rich by sacrificing his profits.

But the question for us here is not, What were the interests of Prussia? but, What was the character of

Mr Carlyle's hero?  We are reviewing a work written by one who, if he be not a great moralist, is
nothing : he has been looking all through history for
a model of a hero-king—he has studied him for
years, painted him for years, and announces loudly,
" Got him at last !—look at him—copy him if you
would be good and great—his doings are as unerring
as a natural law, and when you think him wrong it
is *you* that are mistaken."   And we find at the very
outset that Frederick's dealings are not even those of
the average tradesman, but rather of the huckster.
" Interest in the first place," not justice or fair dealing, is the basis of his commerce with others.

" Magnanimous I can by no means call Friedrich to his
allies and neighbours," says Mr Carlyle, describing a subsequent transaction, "nor even superstitiously veracious, in
this business, but he thoroughly understands, he alone, what
just thing he wants out of it, and what an enormous wigged
mendacity he has got to deal with.   For the rest, he is at the
gaming-table with these sharpers ; their dice all cogged ;—and
he knows it, and ought to profit by his knowledge of it.   And
in short, to win his stake out of that foul weltering melley,
and go home safe with it if he can."

What on earth is a disciple who has been brought
up under a platform of which heroism and veracity,
and confidence in the laws of the universe, are the
main supports, to make of all this?   Not being
" superstitiously veracious," but being a sharper
among sharpers, only cleverer than the rest, and
going safe home with your stake, pronounced by
this authority to be the right course !  Puzzling,

this! And how shall the disciple continue to believe
in a preacher who does not believe his own gospel?

Let it be granted, however, that, if Frederick
must be his hero, Mr Carlyle may be pardoned for
dealing lightly, or even like a partisan, with this
passage of the history ; for it is the very keystone of
the whole : admit that Frederick is wrong here, and
the whole Silesian war falls about our ears, a mere
jumble of battles, fought in the cause of royal brig-
andism, then so common—a "Stygian quagmire,"
having no relation whatever to our old friends the
"Eternal Veracities." But let it be assumed or
believed that Frederick was engaged in a just quarrel, was prosecuting an undoubted right against a
powerful and rapacious enemy, and the fabric is
restored to the proportions of a work of art. We
cannot therefore blame our author altogether if,
after having collected a vast store of materials, and
framed an elaborate plan and scaffolding, he should
have treated this dubious but all important part of
the edifice as Don Quixote treated the pasteboard
visor of his helmet—as something to be taken for
granted and confided in, but not rudely put to proof.
A discreet and shifty partisan, we admit; but a
veracious and incorruptible historian!—"O heavens!"

Having glanced, then, at Frederick's pretext and
his opportunity, let us look at his means for com-
mencing the war. He had inherited from his father

an army which was both strong in numbers in proportion to the population of his kingdom, and far better fitted for the wars of the time than any other then in existence.    Frederick - William had been possessed, among his other eccentricities, by a mania for drill : he instructed his troops frequently in person : and he enforced his regulations for parade and manœuvre by a military code of extreme severity. To a Prussian soldier life was frightfully hard, environed as it was by a quickset of minute rules, the consequence of infringing any of which was terrible ; but the result, though attained at the cost of extreme wretchedness to the individual, was a great perfection of the military machine.    The army could march, manœuvre, and form order of battle, with a precision which would be astonishing now, and with a rapidity which, compared with that of other armies, was quite unrivalled.    Mr Carlyle, who, on the whole perhaps, loves and admires Frederick - William rather more even than the son, his proper hero, has persuaded himself, and tries hard to persuade the world, that this was done from deep design and far - sighted sagacity—that the creator of this formidable force knew well what a superiority in war it would confer on its possessor.    We, on the other hand, attribute its creation to the incessant small activity and petty tyranny that found their fittest field on the parade-ground.    Remembering that the ability shown in the conception and execution of the project was altogether of the drill-sergeant species—that the part of the army on which the old king bestowed his chief favour and affection was the preposterous regiment of giants which he collected with infinite pains from all quarters, and which was immediately disbanded by his successor—and that he neither sought nor found any opportunity of employing the elaborate machine,—we cannot admit that this was other than an accidental direction of the monarch's habitual eccentricity, the result of which was uncommonly fortunate.

The army, then, the pretext for employing it, the will to use it, and the opportunity, were all ready. But the resources of the kingdom were very inadequate to the maintenance of a great war with such a power as Austria. The population of Prussia at that time was less than two millions and a half, and the revenue was about one million sterling. These considerations might have restrained a more experienced potentate; but they were outweighed in Frederick's mind by the ambition to achieve a name.

When the Emperor died, Frederick, then only five months king, did not lose a day in forming his project. For seven weeks he made his preparations, veiling them for a great part of the time with diplomatic craft and mystery; and on the 2d December he set his troops in motion for the invasion of Silesia, intending to hold it altogether if possible, or, at any rate, to obtain other concessions from Austria as the price of its restoration. But it is important to note, as fair evidence of his own opinion as to the justice of his claim, that he kept that claim in the beginning of his enterprise entirely out of sight, proclaiming that he entered Silesia merely to protect the rights of the Queen in that province amidst the perils that threatened the opening of her reign. And he offered, if Silesia were ceded to him (instructing his envoy to accept part if he could not get the whole), to assist the Queen with men and money in supporting both her own right to inherit her dominions, and her husband's nomination to the Kaisership.

Frederick's clutch at Silesia was highly successful. And Mr Carlyle wishes us to think it was not only successful but highly creditable. " A perfectly clear-sighted Friedrich ; able to discriminate shine from substance ; and gravitating always towards the solid, the actual. . . . As supremely adroit, all readers already know him; his appearance what we called starlike,—always something definite, fixed, and lucid in it." Burglary and the picking of pockets may be called " starlike " with equal propriety so long as those felonious operations are " definite, fixed, and lucid." He goes on : " This, his first expedition to Silesia—*a rushing out to seize your own stolen horse, while the occasion answered*—was a voluntary one ; produced, we may say, by Friedrich's own thought and the Invisible Powers. But the rest was all

purely compulsory—to defend the horse he had
seized." From this little parable, under which our
great moralist tries to hide the defects of his client's
title, we may learn how very elastic is that veracity,
on the necessity of making which the ruling prin-
ciple of life he has been often, aforetime, so copi-
ously eloquent. Here is another curious bit of
encomium :—

"For he is full of silent finesse, this young king; soon sees
into his man, and can lead him strange dances on occasion.
In no man is there a plentifuller vein of cunning, nor of a finer
kind — lynx-eyed perspicacity, inexhaustible contrivance,
prompt ingenuity—a man very dangerous to play with at games
of skill. And it is cunning regulated always by a noble sense
of honour, too; instinctively abhorrent of attorneyism and the
swindler element ; a cunning sharp as the vulpine, yet always
strictly human, which is rather beautiful to see. This is one
of Friedrich's marked endowments. Intellect sun-clear, wholly
practical (need not be specially deep), and entirely loyal to the
fact before it ; this—if you add rapidity and energy, prompt
weight of stroke such as was seldom met with—will render a
man very dangerous to his adversary in the game of war."

That Austria should acquiesce in the seizure of
Silesia a moment after she found herself able to
attempt to recover it, is what neither "the gods,"
nor the "Invisible Powers," nor the "Eternal
Veracities," nor any other shifty and inconsistent lawgivers of the universe, could be expected
to require ; and Frederick presently found that he
must prepare "to defend the horse he had seized."
When, to secure his spoils, he prevailed on the

parties to the Pragmatic Sanction to renounce their engagements, the compacts which guaranteed stability and peace were torn up, and there ensued "red ruin and the breaking up of laws." In the ferment of intrigue and rapacity which his act had excited he discerned a recombination of elements hostile to himself, and with characteristic promptitude he prepared to protect his acquisitions by anticipating the attack.

Accordingly, while the Austrians were occupied on the Rhine, he broke out into Bohemia. But neither in this campaign, more than in the last, was there anything to indicate his undeveloped talent for war. He was outgeneralled by the old Austrian Marshal Traun, and compelled to retire into Silesia —confessing in the criticisms which later in life he passed on his own career, that "no general committed more faults than did the King in this campaign."

Frederick would have been well content to remain at peace now on condition of Silesia being secured to him. The historian frequently breaks out into panegyric of his hero's pacific disposition. Here was a young king with a special talent for war and with an army which, conducted by himself, might extend almost indefinitely the dominions of Prussia ; and yet he asked nothing better than simply to be left to the enjoyment of what he had already acquired. It is not easy to join in these praises of his moderation.  His seizure of Silesia had already cost him dear—but it was easier for him to hold this than any other Austrian territory, for the Giant Mountains formed a natural rampart, rendering the advance, and still more the supply, of an enemy's army very difficult and problematical.  He could hope, therefore, to maintain himself there against superior forces; but in Bohemia and Moravia there was no natural barrier short of the Danube that would have given him equal security. It is no wonder, therefore, that he thought rather of securing present conquests than of attempting others. But Mr Carlyle grows pathetic in describing the tribulations and anxieties of this peaceful prince who only wanted to be let alone.  Only let him have his Silesia, and he would gladly betake himself to Sans-Souci to enjoy his flute-playing and the talk of philosophers, and never more trouble his neighbours.  It was so hard, say both the King and his biographer, that these innocent desires should not be gratified, but that perfidious Austria would still at every turn be trying to regain the " horse he had seized."  Now, we should like to ask our historian this question: Suppose Silesia had originally been Frederick's, and that Austria, having exactly such claims as he had put forth, had seized the province—would he have been likely to acquiesce ? or would he not have tried every resource of war and diplomacy to recover it, in spite of a score of extorted treaties ?  We suspect that in such a case his advocate would have been equally eloquent as now in his defence, and certainly on juster grounds.

The peace of Dresden, the result of Frederick's victories in this second Silesian war, by which Silesia was again guaranteed to him, endured for ten years; and for so long the King led the life which amid his wars he had been sighing for. The world, too, eager to know all it could of a warrior already so renowned, and no longer occupied with his military actions only, turned a very curious . scrutinising eye on the Court of Berlin; and there exist, consequently, in public and private records of the time, ample details of the habits and doings of the principal figure. Frederick managed at once to be extremely industrious, and to have plenty of leisure. To do this is to solve one of the most difficult problems of life, and to go far towards finding out the secret of happiness; for it is to impart to daily pleasures the zest of the content which follows from having earned them. He lived a life very much like that of a conscientious country gentleman in England who scrupulously fulfils the duties of the magistracy and the poor-law, manages to the minutest particulars his own property, knows the circumstances and affairs of everybody in his parish, and gives what is left of his time to society and hospitality. But Frederick was far too much addicted to details to be a perfect ruler. It is impos-

sible to combine in the same person the large
general glance of the statesman, and the micros-
copic scrutiny of the ordinary man of business; and
Frederick's faculties as a ruler must have suffered
from his habits of superintending in their minute
particulars petty affairs. The practice of the Caliph
Haroun Alraschid, of going forth at night with his
officers, Giaffir and Mesrour, to observe secretly, and
in disguise, the manner in which the laws were exe-
cuted in the city of Bagdad, and to remedy isolated
acts of injustice, may be supposed to have exercised
a wholesome, if a desultory, influence on the corrupt
judicature of an Eastern community. But this kind
of interference would have a very different effect
in a civilised country, where established laws were
administered by trained and respectable functionaries.
We fear, then, that we cannot join in the applause
which Mr Carlyle demands for his hero, when he
records such exceptional instances of royal interference as that of the case of Miller Arnold. It probably
did (even if the King's decision were just, which is
by no means evident) more harm than good. The
true secret of ruling, in any position of authority, is
not in doing everything yourself, but in making
every subordinate perform his share of the labour,
and take his share of the responsibility. In the
navy they call a captain who does everybody's business a G.C.B.—Gunner, Carpenter, and Boatswain—
Frederick's fault was that he was a G.C.B.

Socially, he had talents, conversational powers, and a fondness for discussion, whether light or philosophic, which would have made him one of the most agreeable men of his time, but for a marked malevolence which rendered the atmosphere around him insecure and capricious. His biting propensity . showed itself equally to his brother monarchs and to his humblest dependants. It was partly owing to this that he passed through life solitary, though in the midst of courts or of armies, with many faithful subjects, but with no friend. Politically, he was rather astute than wise, for his mind had not the elevation of view and grandeur of purpose essential to wisdom. His was always a peddling policy, aiming at mere material advantages, and sticking at nothing in order to compass them.

All through the Seven Years' War the fame of Frederick constantly increased, though fortune, sometimes raising, sometimes depressing him, left still the balance constantly against him. In many skilful marches, and amid many failures—in the terrible defeat of Kunersdorf and the victory of Liegnitz—he showed still the same indomitable persistence. It is a picture which wants only a high just cause in the background to render it heroic ; failing that, we have the image only of a valiant bull-dog, who having stolen a bone, fights for it, lies gasping and growling on it, shakes his torn ears, winks his bleeding eyes, and will surrender it only with his life.

When matters were at their worst with him they began to mend. In 1762 his great enemy, the Czarina Catherine, died, and her successors ceased hostilities against him. In the following year Austria and France, wearied of fruitless campaigns and the infliction of mutual damage, made peace with Prussia, and the last of Frederick's wars ended. He remained a conqueror, not so much by reason of any signal successes, for the later campaigns of the war had been generally disastrous to him, but because the league against him, in the absence of a supreme directing spirit, could not bear the stress of a protracted and exhausting struggle. He had made good his hold on his booty—he and Prussia had gained a military reputation transcendent in that age — and henceforth there was a new German Power standing in the front rank in Europe.

Frederick was fifty-one when his wars were finished. For twenty-three years he continued to rule in the country which his martial genius and superhuman determination had raised to greatness. Excepting the partition of Poland, there was no act of this part of his reign to call for special notice. The great soldiers who had gathered round him in the stirring portion of his career were dead—Schwerin, Winterfeld, Keith, slain in battle—Ziethen laid in old age in a peaceful grave; and the King was not of a nature to supply by new intimacies the loss of those paladins of his youth. Aged, solitary, and cheerless, he met his end sternly and drearily, a few years before the old order of things passed away and the new era commenced with the French Revolution.

Widely different opinions will always exist respecting Carlyle's merits as an historian. All the world is familiar with his oddities and his genius, and the circle must be dull and unlettered indeed where there cannot be found critics ready to extol or to denounce him. Setting aside the mere quips and cranks of his style as what no longer offends us, there is graver reason for objection in the prevailing tone of grotesqueness which marks his treatment of events and characters. No historian was ever more picturesque, none ever studied more how, by carefully chosen or carefully invented epithets, to give force and individuality to a scene or a character. But the result of habitually treating everything and everybody, except a few oddly selected heroes and their doings, in a jeering, semi-contemptuous way, is to produce an effect which resembles life only in the same way as the work of medieval carvers in gargoyles, brackets, and church-doors resembles nature. Everywhere there is exaggeration and distortion, as if we were looking at things in a convex mirror. But in parting with the history we prefer rather to touch on those characteristics which spring from the force and fertility of his genius. The jeering tone is, after all, only a strange habit,

not of heart, but of fancy ; for no reader can doubt
that the writer in his most contemptuous mood still
wishes heartily well to humanity, and studies with
a kindly as well as lively interest the faults and
failings of his fellow-men,—just as it is the humour
of some good-natured people to do favours in a rough
way, as if their benevolence needed cynicism on the
outside to excuse it.    Throughout this extensive
work there is the same unwearied imagination at
work, seeking to penetrate into the nature of men
and things, and imparting to them life and motion.
But let those who admire Carlyle's style, and covet
a share of his celebrity, beware of making him their
model.    No great writer is more easy and more
perilous to imitate.    Nothing but derision can await
the disciple who may attempt to charm the public
by reproducing those singularities which only the
most affluent imagination and rare descriptive power
could exalt into distinctions.

   We sometimes think that if he had begun his
career by a plain statement of his belief, instead of
leaving it to be inferred from the dark hints of prophecy and denunciation, his influence would have
been more lasting, and his course far clearer. All
his aberrations seem traceable to his habit of
thinking in metaphor, which is putting the flower
in place of the root.    For the purposes of illus-
trating and adorning, there is nothing like metaphor ; it is as a stained window, throwing not

merely light, but coloured light; but to begin
with it—to make your basement of painted glass—
this is bad architecture; and the fact that literary
or philosophical edifices have been built so, only
proves that they are more specious than solid. We
do not think it would have been so difficult to state
the premises of his creed in plain English. Let us
try :—We are called to this visible world from another unseen one, whither we shall return; and we
walk here furnished with what we find and with
what we bring. We find bodily senses and capa-
cities of pain and pleasure; we bring spirit with
its light of conscience. Thus equipped, humanity
divides itself into three grand classes. There are
those who make what they bring from the eternal
unseen subservient to what they find in the temporary visible; these are the Devil's messengers
and Beelzebub-worshippers of Carlyle. There are
those who, though feebly bound to this world, yet
bear but a faint impress of the other—to whom life
is but a picture, having no earnestness or reality—
the Shams, Ineptitudes, and Phantasm - Captains.
And there are those to whom this life is intensely
earnest, not because of what they find in it, but
because of what they bring to it; who, in their
passage across this bridge of time, walk always
environed by the laws which belong to no time,
linked to what is above by reverence, and to what
is akin by justice; to whom pleasure is pleasant,

and pain suffering, but to whom right is better than pleasure, wrong less endurable than pain;—these are the Heroes.   And, as the men, so are their works.   Everything produced or producible by the two first classes is essentially a thing of time—a thing either evil and an injury, or futile and a hindrance, bearing in itself the element of decay;—while all that the others, the salt of the earth, do is vital and beneficent, because mingled with something that is divine.   This is intelligible—this is noble; it is incontrovertible, because it is in unison with every man's conscience when conscience is permitted to be heard.   Apply it to any of Carlyle's doctrines, and we think it will illustrate their course and indicate their variations.   Out of this simple theory grows in practice the multiform aspect of humanity, and out of the metaphors which encumber it grow the cloud-castles of Carlyle.

PRINTED BY WILLIAM BLACKWOOD AND SONS.

www.ingramcontent.com/pod-product-compliance
Lightning Source LLC
Chambersburg PA
CBHW032154010726
47493CB00008BA/2690